Praise for *Marshmallow*

'*Kokomo* got rave reviews, and this is as good'
Weekend Australian

'I'm always looking for novels that make me laugh as well as think and feel. *Marshmallow* achieved all of these things'
The Age

'Powerful'
Marie Claire

'Hannan combines a sharp wit with great emotional tenderness. The result is a heartbreaking, surprisingly funny story about grief and love; about facing darkness and finding hope'
Diana Reid, author of *Love & Virtue* and *Seeing Other People*

'An exquisitely crafted and enthralling portrait of the shadows that form after unthinkable loss. The way these five friends move through earth-shattering grief together and alone is deeply moving and utterly captivating'
Rhett Davis, author of *Hovering*

'A propulsive, big-hearted and compassionate exploration of grief, love and friendship'
Jessica Stanley, author of *A Great Hope*

'A beautiful study of the physicality of grief and the complexity of family and class. Somehow Hannan balances these themes skilfully into a hopeful book with friendship at its heart'
Alice Bishop, author of *A Constant H*

T0359611

Praise for *Kokomo*

'With *Kokomo* as a starting point, one can only imagine what heights [Hannan] will soar to next'
The Guardian

'This superbly written book will appeal to readers of Zadie Smith and Jennifer Down'
Books+Publishing

'Ironic, smart and witty'
Sydney Morning Herald

'Tender and brutal'
Sunday Age

'Both a beautiful examination of a mother–daughter relationship and a funny coming-of-age tale about a woman in her thirties'
Herald Sun

'An emotive look at whether we can ever truly know someone'
Elle

'Hannan's use of language is vivid and visceral, lavish with colour'
ArtsHub

'*Kokomo* is a book in which many young(ish) readers will see their own lives and interior landscapes mirrored, but it's so much more than that. It's about those things that bust generational boundaries: love, family, friendship, home'
The Conversation

'[Hannan's] originality took my breath away'
Newtown Review of Books

'A thoughtful novel of fractured family relationships and the unseen impact of family secrets'
Canberra Times

'There are many striking passages, brilliantly executed scenes, and gorgeous uses of the written word in this book . . . and it's easy to see why Hannan won the coveted Unpublished Manuscript Award at 2019's Victorian Premier's Literary Awards'
Alison Huber, Readings

'Smart and sensitive, punctuated with moments of real humour . . . This is first rate fiction from a writer to watch'
Simon McDonald, Potts Point Bookshop

'Hannan, in fresh, unpretentious prose, showcases a frankness and tenderness when dealing with her characters, who are fully realised and feel instantly familiar'
Ben Hunter, Booktopia

'This debut heralds an exciting new Australian voice'
Anna Krien, author of *Night Games* and *Act of Grace*

'An intricate, glittering gem. One of the best debuts in years'
Mark Brandi, author of *Wimmera*, *The Rip* and *The Others*

'Crystalline, genuine, heartbreaking and powerful'
Sarah Schmidt, author of *See What I Have Done* and *Blue Hour*

'So full of life, on each page there are tiny moments of delight, irreverence, tenderness'
J.P. Pomare, author of *Call Me Evie*, *The Last Guests* and *The Wrong Woman*

'This is smart, raw, tender fiction that feels as real as life'
Ronnie Scott, author of *The Adversary*

Victoria Hannan
marshmallow

 hachette
AUSTRALIA

This project is supported by the Victorian Government through Creative Victoria.

Supported by the Copyright Agency's Cultural Fund.

First published in Australia and New Zealand in 2022
by Hachette Australia
(an imprint of Hachette Australia Pty Limited)
Gadigal Country, Level 17, 207 Kent Street, Sydney, NSW 2000
www.hachette.com.au

This edition published in 2023

Hachette Australia acknowledges and pays our respects to the past, present and future Traditional Owners and Custodians of Country throughout Australia and recognises the continuation of cultural, spiritual and educational practices of Aboriginal and Torres Strait Islander peoples. Our head office is located on the lands of the Gadigal people of the Eora Nation.

A catalogue record for this book is available from the National Library of Australia

ISBN: 978 0 7336 4951 6 (paperback)

Cover design by Alissa Dinallo
Cover photograph courtesy of Chantal Convertini
Author photograph courtesy of Shelley Horan
Typeset in Simoncini Garamond by Bookhouse
Printed and bound in Australia by McPherson's Printing Group

The paper this book is printed on is certified against the Forest Stewardship Council® Standards. McPherson's Printing Group holds FSC® chain of custody certification SA-COC-005379. FSC® promotes environmentally responsible, socially beneficial and economically viable management of the world's forests.

You are neither here nor there,
A hurry through which known and strange things pass
As big soft buffetings come at the car sideways
And catch the heart off guard and blow it open.

'Postscript', Seamus Heaney

One

HE HELD HIS BREATH. HELD it because in the seconds between breathing in and breathing out, there was silence. He couldn't hear the buzzing of electricity in the wires that snaked through the walls. He couldn't hear the water moving through the pipes. He couldn't hear the gas doing whatever it was gas did. Bubbling? Sliding? Floating? It didn't matter because he couldn't hear it.

He couldn't hear his heart racing in his chest.

The absence of Claire was the absence of noise, too: of air passing through nostrils, past the pharynx, through bronchioles and back. The sniffing and snuffling sounds of sleep.

For that one moment, the world was still. The world was quiet.

Then his chest started to hurt and he exhaled, one long sigh punctuated by the sound of four paws landing on the duvet.

A gentle thud: Crunchie's little footsteps flattening feathers, her purr, then a squeaky meow that would be relentless now, increasing in volume until a spoonful of raw meat was splattered into her bowl and hoovered into her smelly mouth.

If Claire were there, still asleep beside him, he'd get to lie unbothered as Crunchie gently kneaded the ends of her blonde bob, getting closer and closer to her scalp, her claws eventually making contact with skin. But Claire was gone. He wondered if she'd got home late and left early, or hadn't come home at all. Sometimes, lately, he'd woken to see her creeping in or creeping out, not wanting to wake him – but for his sake or hers? Some mornings he'd wake to her fingers tapping tapping tapping on her keyboard. But not today. Today Al was aware of the absence of things, the volume of the missing.

He reached up and grabbed the ginger lump of Crunchie's body, pulling her close to his bare chest. He kissed the top of her head as she wriggled in his arms, excited. His movement meant breakfast was near.

AL FILLED THE kettle, turned it on, listened to the whine of the elements as they warmed, the bubble of the water as it boiled. Had it always been that loud? The aggravation hit him with the ferocity of the flying chairs in the YouTube bar fight he'd watched the previous evening. Danny had mentioned it at the pub and they all sat around a phone and watched as a Greek restaurant

2

erupted with men punching and kicking each other, hurting each other the way men sometimes do.

Beside the fridge, her meat swallowed in two big gulps, Crunchie's biscuits were being broken in half by her tiny molars. A few streets over, a train honked at the level crossing, two long honks followed by two shorter ones, and Al wished for silence. Steam gathered in the kettle and Al, his skin alive with impatience and irritation, flicked it off and abandoned the two scoops of coffee that sat in the bottom of the glass plunger.

In the shower, he turned the taps on; the pipes squealed and shuddered. He angled the shower head as high as it would go but he still didn't fit under it properly. He had to duck when he wanted to wash his face, his hair, the back of his long neck. This house, like most of the houses he'd lived in throughout his life, was not built for men like him. Sometimes it felt as if the world was not built for men like him. He felt like a giant.

Al had learned early that his height was interesting to other people. He'd lost count of the number of times he was asked 'How's the weather up there?' or the number of people who assumed he was good at basketball. Once, a table of men chanted 'BFG' at him. He used to laugh as if each time he heard these comments was the first. Lately, though, he'd stopped pretending. There had been a few occasions, always late at night, almost always in the city, where other men had seen him and assumed that, like them, he was itching for a fight. They'd bump into him, knock his drink out of his hand, ask him what his problem was. Al could practically see them twitching, their bodies full of feelings they didn't know what to do with. Somewhere – or from someone – they'd learned that punching or getting punched would help.

Maybe those guys were on to something, Al thought, recalling the video of the fight, the way the chair had cracked on a man's shoulder. Maybe the splitting of lips, the taste of blood, knuckles bruised by the sharp bones of a nose, the long bones of a jaw, would fix the feelings he didn't know what to do with. He felt a tingle on the skin of his arms, in the muscles of his hands as he soaped his armpits and chest with a squidge of Claire's expensive body wash. He turned the taps off – too tight, just because it felt good – and wrapped himself in a towel.

He dried his back, his chest. As he moved through to the bedroom he left wet footprints on the polished floorboards of their expensive rental. He dried his arms, torso, his legs, his cock and balls, then sat on the edge of the bed. Everything felt like hard work today. Everything felt like it was tugging at his skin, like Crunchie's claws needling and needling at him.

He picked through the stash of skincare on the dresser and found the moisturiser Claire had bought for him. He rubbed it into his hands first and then into the skin on his face – Claire had told him he had an oily T-zone, a dry something or other else – and as he rubbed it into the dark circles under his eyes, an image came to him in a flash: the crunch of his fist against a mouth, of soft lips slicing open, the warm trickle of blood. The rush of it, the colour, left Al just as quickly as it had come.

He looked at the time. Seven fifteen. Seven fifteen. Seven sixteen. It was Friday. It was November second. Summer had come early and it would be a warmer than usual day, but that didn't explain the sweat beading across his lip, across his forehead. Al knew there was a reasonable explanation as to why his heart was beating so fast, why everything felt so loud and so hard. Tomorrow would be a year since it happened; tomorrow was one whole year of these feelings rising in him too easily, too often. Of them accumulating. Of them combining like a dangerous cocktail, like a high school science experiment about to fizz over, about to smash the thin glass of a beaker. But knowing where they came from didn't make them go away, didn't stop them from getting into his bones somehow. He thought of the frogs in slowly boiling water and felt envy. At least there was an end in sight for them. November second.

He shook his body, shook his head, as though shaking would be enough to dislodge something, to ease the tension, open a valve and let the steam out, but it wasn't. Instead, he stood and shoved it all into a pair of jocks, a pair of black jeans, a clean enough t-shirt, a jacket. Instead, he thought about the only thing that would fix this, that would sand down those sharp edges. He looked at the time. Seven nineteen. Too early for a drink. Too early.

THE TRAIN WAS already on the platform when he arrived at Northcote station. He squeezed through the closing doors.

A greasy-haired man rolled his eyes at Al, furious at the space he took up. Al let himself imagine ripping the man's sporty backpack off his back, thick straps tugged down over his shoulders, and chucking it out the doors when they next opened. The man's arms flailing, the look on his little sparrow face as he sprinted to get to it before the doors closed. But if Al did that, there'd probably be cops waiting for him on the platform at the next station. Someone would film it and he'd end up all over social media. He knew the way things worked.

Instead, he said excuse me, excuse me, sorry, excuse me as he pushed past the man, past the other bodies packed near the door, to stand in the near-empty aisle, towering over the people sitting. He looked down. There were people dressed in various levels of business attire, necks crooked, spines curved, scrolling and scrolling through their phones, not stopping to read the words, barely even looking at the pictures.

The train rattled south towards the city. He held on to the long yellow bar with one hand, tapped his jacket pocket, his t-shirt pocket, his jeans pockets, searching for a familiar shape. He swapped hands, did it all again, as if his left was more likely to pick up the shape of his earphones under cotton or denim than his right. He had his wallet, his work pass. He refused to be one of those people who wore theirs on the train – their full names and ugly ID photos facing outwards. Did they want everyone to know how boring their jobs were? To know their names? To google them and discover that their lives outside of work were boring too? Photos of breakfasts and doggo cuddles on their Instagram profiles. No thank you.

On the rare occasion that he and Claire caught the train to work together, when she didn't leave at five-thirty to spend too long at the gym before spending too long at the office, he'd chastise her for wearing her work pass clipped to her trousers (she, at least, looked good in her photo), the red Strong, King and Noble logo in the corner. She claimed that wearing it meant she knew where it was at all times, a point she made for his benefit, as he would often leave his at home – in the back pocket of yesterday's jeans, wedged inside a book as a makeshift bookmark, down the back of the bedside table where it'd been chucked – or, worse, he'd lose it on the way home after a few too many drinks at the pub after work. Ali Nazari, Senior Digital Producer, lost out there in the world somewhere. Each time he showed up at work without it, he'd have to text a colleague to come down and get him, or slip in through the barriers behind someone he knew. Each reissue was docked from his pay.

He checked his pockets again. Keys. Phone. No headphones.

'Fuck's sake,' he hissed under his breath. Someone nearby looked up at him and then away quickly. Fucking idiot, he thought. Forgetting his headphones was a sure way to ruin an already shitty day. He stared out the window, furious. He wanted to kick the metal part of the seat, throw his phone at the glass, but he didn't. He just watched the houses whizz past. A blur of red brick, green prickly pears, wood, metal. The train slowed as it rolled into the next station, and the faces of the people waiting to board sharpened into focus.

They filed in one by one, pushing their way into the confined space. A man and a woman stood too close to Al, too close to each other. They were together, it seemed.

Al watched the man as he tapped and flicked the screen of his Apple Watch. He had jowly cheeks that, in a few years, would become one with his neck, a curly patch of dark hair that was thinning on top, an invisible yet somehow perceptible dampness to him. He gave off the vibe of the person no one wanted to be stuck next to at a dinner.

'Maybe I should get an iWatch,' said the woman, reaching over to touch the small, smooth screen.

'It's actually called an Apple Watch,' the man said, snatching his arm away from her. His girlfriend looked hurt, but he didn't notice; he just flicked and tapped. 'I'm so senior now I have people after me all day. Even with a PA, I can barely keep up.'

Al rolled his eyes so far back in their sockets that all he could see was darkness.

'I get a lot of emails too,' she said under her breath, but the boyfriend wasn't listening.

Al hated him. Wholly and instantly. He looked at the woman: Caroline Davis – her ID card was clipped to the waist of her beige pencil skirt. The photo was an old one, he thought unkindly. In it, she had colour in her cheeks and her hair was dyed, straightened.

There, in person, she looked small, thin, a little hunched. Sad, Al thought; she looked sad.

Out the window, green and brown flashed by, the colours of Australian suburbia. He wanted to scream.

'So will you come to my place tonight?' Caroline asked hopefully.

'Why don't you come to mine again?' the man suggested, and Al heard her sigh.

'I need clothes.' She pursed her lips, looked down at her outfit as if to illustrate a point.

'Go to yours after work, get some clothes, come to mine.'

'Okay,' she said, resigned.

Al was tempted to lean over and whisper, 'Leave him,' but didn't. He stood and listened to them make a plan for the evening. He would go for a run. She would cook.

Al had often joked that the only reason he and Claire moved in together so quickly six years ago was because they both hated what Claire called 'couple's logistics' – the constant back and forth, packing bags of underwear, pyjamas, a toothbrush, the politics of what you were allowed to leave behind, a game of tennis that no one won. Claire didn't have time for it. Al didn't have the patience. (In truth though, they couldn't get enough of each other. Their second date lasted forty-eight hours. In the first two months of their relationship, they barely spent a night apart. In those early years, his chest ached when he thought of her.)

Al's hand felt clammy against the metal railing. He rested his forehead against it, closed his eyes and thought about places he'd rather be: still in bed; in a darkened movie theatre; at the pub; on a tropical island, learning to survive Tom Hanks–style. There it'd be quiet. November. November second. The date buzzed in his head, caused the muscles in his neck and shoulders to tighten.

Finally. The train pulled into the city station.

The platform was already full of people. More spilled out from the doors when they opened. Al waited for the carriage to all but empty before he followed, almost walking slap-bang into the man with the backpack who'd stopped dead in his tracks. Al swallowed his anger, tamped it down.

Once through the barriers, he launched himself across the road, weaved between stopped cars and morning commuters, and rounded the corner, crossed the square. It wasn't far. He swiped his card at the security gates in the foyer, swiped it again in the lift, pressed three, pressed the close-doors button to avoid sharing the space with someone, to avoid any small talk or eye contact, to get up to his desk faster. He pressed it repeatedly. The lift doors slid shut.

AL SAT DOWN at his desk, the feeling of pins pricking his insides, pricking his skin. He pushed aside a plate of half-eaten cake from yesterday's birthday afternoon tea, its icing glossy with grease, its crumbs air-dried. He hadn't spoken to anyone at the celebration; he'd stood on the edge of conversations, picking at the flesh of the cake.

He pressed a key and waited for his monitor to come to life. He mistyped his password, swore, got it right the second time. On the screen was an overdue, unfinished scope of work he'd stared at for a few hours every day that week. He closed it, opened a browser, went to Google. He entered his usual search term: 'Woodward marshmallow'.

He read the same articles with the same photo of the smiling boy. Nothing new. Nothing damning. Yet it brought him no peace, no solace. It didn't change the fact of what had happened nearly a year ago.

He knew he should stop and look through his inbox, write a to-do list, get his shit together. But he couldn't. He couldn't stop looking, couldn't stop venturing off on his now-daily anxiety tour of the internet. He opened a new tab and went to Facebook. He hated Facebook but it never failed to serve him in this singular purpose.

When she'd first started doing it, Al had detested Bec's public grieving, the performance of it. But in the last year, he'd visited her profile more regularly than he would've cared to admit. He typed in Bec's name and scrolled back down her wall, past shared memes about having young toddlers, past photos of her and the girls at brunch together. Al didn't know how their lives, bonded forever by loss, could look so different.

Then there it was. Re-posted every thirty-first of December like clockwork. A photo, her name, the few short years she had lived: Carmen Laing, 24/6/1982–31/12/1999.

The photo was from the New Year's Eve party where it had happened. It was overexposed, the flash too close, just hints of her freckles, the bright browns of her eyes, her teeth six months out of braces. She was smiling, her hair still damp, curly from the plait she'd undone, the elastic around her wrist. Even now, he could remember the smell of her shampoo. He could remember feeling a pang of longing; that was all he knew of love back then.

And he could remember what they'd said about her at the funeral: she was a nice girl, she excelled at maths, was a good long-distance runner, wanted to be a nurse, was popular, well-mannered. Tragic.

He'd heard the word 'tragic' a lot in his life; it seemed to follow him like a stray dog, like a bad smell. When they met, he'd told Claire the whole sob story about his parents but never about Carmen. It felt like one piece of baggage too many. For all these years, he'd let her believe he hated New Year's Eve because he was a grouch. It was easier than telling her the truth.

Al stared at the photo, at Carmen's smile and at the two figures in the background. Jason in a Nirvana t-shirt, blond hair down to his shoulders. The other, his face half in shadow, so tall even at eighteen, was Al.

His brain toggled between the two deaths. They had nothing in common except him. He was the common thread.

He tried to breathe. Tried to get air into his lungs. His skin felt so itchy he wanted to be rid of it. To peel it back and throw it in the bin next to his desk. Instead, he stood, turned and walked out of the office.

'IF THIS IS about tonight, I will not be accepting excuses,' Zahra said when she answered.

'I need to see you,' Al said. He was on the street already, heading in the direction of her office.

'I'm almost at work,' she complained.

Al tapped the button at the crossing four times, then four times more. Anxiety roared through his body.

'Please,' he said. He didn't want to beg but he would. He'd do anything.

'Now?'

'Now,' Al said, and he jogged across the road without waiting for the lights. 'That place on Collins Street you like.' He hung up, not giving her a chance to say no.

At the cafe, Al found a table by the window, sat with his phone unlocked, signed into Slack, into his email. A familiar ruse to make it look like he was still working, even though he was away from his desk.

He was halfway through a coffee when Zahra arrived: her hair piled up on her head in a huge bun, her fringe a perfect straight line. He stood, they hugged. He became aware of his t-shirt sticking to his back, the sweat slicked across his forehead. Zahra took a napkin off the table and wiped her hands as they sat down.

'Sorry,' he said, and Zahra shrugged, unperturbed as always. She caught the attention of a waiter and ordered a coffee seemingly in one graceful motion.

'I need to hear the thing,' Al asked when Zahra turned her attention to him.

'Hello, cousin, it's nice to see you too,' she said sarcastically. 'I'm fine, thanks for asking.'

'Sorry,' he said again, trying to quash the frustration he felt rising in him.

'What happened?' she asked, pouring them both a glass of water and sliding his into his hands.

'Nothing really,' he said. He slumped back in his chair, then sat forward again. He couldn't sit still, couldn't get comfortable. 'But also, you know.'

'It's okay,' she said kindly. 'I know what day it is tomorrow. It was bound to bring stuff up. So here's the bit where I tell you –' Zahra paused, looked down at her phone buzzing with messages, meeting alerts. All the things she had to do on November second. How was anyone supposed to do anything on November second? November third? On New Year's Eve? He rubbed his face, then let his eyes wander around the cafe before coming back to rest on his cousin, her sleeveless top, her tailored pants and designer handbag. He didn't know how she managed to keep it together. Where did she put all the feelings? 'Here's the bit where I tell you it wasn't your fault.' Zahra let it sink in, then said it again. 'It wasn't your fault.'

Al felt the pangs of guilt and shame and missing and emptiness and regret scratching at him. He jiggled his knee up and down, nervous energy pulsing through him.

'Fucking hell,' he said glumly. 'I just can't stop thinking about –'

Zahra reached across the table and squeezed his arm, cutting him off mid-sentence. 'It wasn't your fault, Al,' she said. 'Not what happened a year ago, not what happened twenty years ago.'

'But . . .' he began. 'The . . .' He paused. Whispered: 'The drugs.'

'Coincidence,' Zahra said, squeezing his arm harder.

'But . . .' he tried again – if she could only see it from his perspective. He'd lived with Zahra and her family since they were both three. She was like a sister to him. And, despite their closeness in age, sometimes like a mother too. 'But what if Carmen took a pill after all and that's why she was on the roof, that's why she fell?'

'Then it would've shown up in the autopsy.'

'What if they made a mistake?'

'Ali, what are you going to do? Get them to exhume Carmen's body? Come on.' Zahra sighed. 'You bringing some ecstasy to a party almost twenty years ago didn't make your friend fall off the roof. You smoking a tiny joint at a birthday party a year ago didn't make that poor little boy choke.' She was getting angry now, almost breathless because of it. 'They were accidents. They're terrible and tragic and awful but sometimes terrible, tragic, awful things happen.' She was gripping his arm even harder now. 'None of it is your fault.'

She looked at her phone, drained the rest of her coffee.

'The date, the anniversary. It just brings up so much new shit,' he said. Looking down, he realised that as Zahra was talking, he'd been shredding his napkin. It sat in pieces on the table in front of him.

'It's not new shit. It's the same shit all mixed up together,' she said. 'You're still wading through it. You're like that horse from *The NeverEnding Story*.' She looked at her phone again; he could tell she had to go, to get back to work, but knew she'd stay with him as long as he needed her to.

'Artax,' he said, remembering the scene they'd both sobbed through as kids.

'That's it. You're sinking in the Swamps of Sadness. If you're not careful, you're going to go under.' Her phone screen lit up again. 'You need to talk to Claire, talk to Nathan, Ev and Annie.'

Al winced at the thought of talking to Annie. She was, at least she used to be, somehow both the warmest and the bossiest person he'd ever known. (She'd once convinced him to drive her on a four-hour round trip to Shepparton to pick up a vase she'd bought on Facebook Marketplace when both Claire and Nathan were working. They ate sausage rolls by the lake in Nagambie, sang Wings songs the whole way there.) Annie used to be so much fun. Now, she was like a ghost of herself. What would he even say?

'No one knows what you're going through better than the four other people who were there,' Zahra continued. 'And they're all probably feeling like shit today too. Have you thought any more about seeing a doctor and getting a mental health plan?'

He hadn't told Zahra about the trip to the emergency room; he'd thought he was having a heart attack but it turned out to be a panic attack. She looked at him as if anticipating a rebuttal, an excuse. But he knew she was right.

'I will,' he said. 'I promise I will. Thank you for meeting me.' He stood.

'I'll see you tonight?' She slipped her phone into her bag, picked her jacket up by its collar, noticed the blank look on his face. 'Come on, Al. Dinner at Javeed's new apartment?'

'Oh god, I'm not coming to that.'

'Non-negotiable. Bibi will finally put that curse on you if you don't.'

Al smiled at that. Their grandmother had been threatening them all with a curse since childhood. A curse for misbehaviour. A curse for talking back. A curse for not eating their vegetables. Every time, a look that said, *Haven't we been through enough?* There were times in Al's life when he wondered whether a curse hadn't been placed on him already.

He groaned. 'Fine.'

'I'll text you the details,' she said, knowing he'd be too lazy to search for them and would text her for them anyway.

They hugged.

'Thank you,' he said.

'You're welcome.' She turned to leave then turned back. 'And, Al?' she said. 'Not your fault.'

He pulled his mouth into a straight-lipped smile and nodded, but they both knew he didn't believe her. He paid for the coffees and pushed his way back through the guts of the city to his office.

AL SAT AT the back of the meeting room, his laptop on his lap. He'd sweated through his t-shirt jogging back to the office and everyone had noticed: the big V of it on his front, his back, the circle patches around his armpits.

'Are you okay?' Katrina whispered when she saw him come in, moisture dripping down his temples. He felt it turn cold in the air-conditioning.

'Yep,' he'd said. 'Sorry I'm late.' In his breathlessness, it was all he could manage. He felt everyone's eyes on him as he took the seat next to her, the only one spare in the room.

The guy presenting had paused while Al got settled but resumed clicking through his slides. Something about website data, which stories got the most traction, content directives for the next quarter. Blah blah blah. It was all stuff any digital producer worth their salt could find out for themselves. Al would be able to in seconds if someone bothered to send him the login details he'd asked for months ago. He felt his leg going again, his knee jiggling. Out of the corner of his eye, he saw Katrina look at him and he stopped moving, letting the energy course through his veins instead, letting it build and build.

He opened his laptop, angled the screen just out of Katrina's view. Bec's Facebook page was still there. He scrolled back through time. Another New Year's Eve, another tribute.

He flicked back and forth between the Facebook page and articles about the little boy. Two tragic events. The smiling faces of two kids he'd loved. Two kids he'd lost. He heard Zahra's voice in his head: *Not your fault. Not your fault.* He repeated it to himself again and again, in her voice, in his. He screamed it. He screamed it until the words were indecipherable, until there was only noise in his head. So much noise. He snapped his laptop shut and, for the second time that day, he stood and walked out of the room.

Two

CLAIRE READ AND REREAD THE job description on the plane. She
sat in business class with all the men in suits. The one next to
her had the morning's broadsheet spread across his tray table. He
held the finance pages wide open, one hand against the window,
one hand too close to her chest. She sat stiff, upright. He moved
only when breakfast arrived: smoked salmon, poached eggs. She
drank black coffee, ate nothing.

She'd taken most of the day off work and told them she had
appointments. She told Al she was flying up for a meeting, that
she'd be back late. Not to wait up.

On past trips, he'd flown up to meet her. After a long day of
meetings, she'd find him waiting in the hotel bar for her. His
kind face beaming when he saw her arrive. They'd spend the
weekend together always in the same way: a hotel room with

a view of the harbour, a dinner of small plates and expensive wine, the clifftop walk between Bondi and Bronte the next day. They'd wade down the weedy steps at the ocean pool cut right out of the rock, the waves crashing over the edge. Later, they'd eat room service burgers and drink beer from the minibar, try to have sex in the big, beautiful shower.

'Porn makes it look easy,' Al had said the first time they tried.

Those trips were from before. Before. This time, she'd told Al that they couldn't spend the weekend in Sydney. Not this weekend. She wasn't sure what was a lie and what was the truth anymore.

When the wheels hit the tarmac Claire felt a tickle of something. It wasn't nerves, though that would be a natural response before an interview for what appeared to be the job of her dreams. Rather, it felt like possibility. Potential. Freedom? (From what? she asked herself, but trying to determine an answer made her brain feel fuzzy, made it buzz in black and white like TV static.)

'THERE SHE IS,' Helen said as Claire exited the lift. Her arms were already outstretched for a hug. 'Everyone's excited to meet you.'

They broke from the hug and Helen held Claire at arm's length, hands planted firmly on her shoulders. She squeezed them as if to say, *Here we go*.

They started with a tour of the office. Claire guessed her mentor was in her late fifties now, still walking around in immaculate Louboutins, her hair pulled back in a tight ponytail, no hint of grey. She was the country's most powerful environmental lawyer, putting together a class action against the government. It helped, everyone knew, that Helen's second husband was Gerry McManus. If rumours were to be believed, he'd agreed to the creation of Helen's team as part of the pre-nup. Helen was a woman who always got what she wanted, and now she wanted Claire to help her 'save the world'.

'Your office will have a view a bit like this,' Helen said with a glint in her eye.

Through the floor-to-ceiling window, between two tall buildings, Claire saw the metal arch of the Sydney Harbour Bridge, the sparkle of the water, a tip of a sail of the Opera House. It was almost enough to make her believe in magic.

'Not bad,' she said.

She'd breezed through the first two phone interviews. Ninety minutes each. The more she heard about the job, the more she felt Helen was right, that it was too good to refuse. Helen had been trying to find a way to get Claire to work with her for the better part of a decade. The timing was never quite right, the job never quite right. Previously, Claire couldn't justify the move. Now she thought about it constantly. About where else she could go, about who else she could be when she was nine hundred kilometres away. About what it would feel like to be anywhere but at home underneath the weight of Al's pain.

At the conclusion of the tour, Helen led Claire to a boardroom. Through the wall of glass, Claire saw three lawyers: sharp suits, neat hair. They stopped chatting between them when they saw Claire and Helen coming. One smiled at her warmly. Claire dug a nail into the webbing between her thumb and index finger.

The interview lasted an hour, during which Claire was calm, clear and concise. She didn't break a sweat. Helen didn't say as much but Claire knew by the look on her face that the job was hers if she wanted it.

They went to an early lunch in a restaurant with dimmed amber light, illuminated bottles of wine behind glass, a long raw bar full of sea creatures on ice. Thinking of the slimy oysters made Claire's guts churn. She sipped from her glass of sparkling water and noticed that her hands were shaking. She tried to remember the last thing she'd eaten: a soy yoghurt when she got home past midnight – before that, who knew?

Helen ordered two glasses of Veuve while Claire looked at the menu.

'It's on Gerry,' Helen said, 'so go wild.'

Spatchcock, pork cutlet, a hundred-and-twenty-dollar Wagyu filet mignon. Who ate like this? But the restaurant was full, soundtracked by the clinking of wineglasses and the laughter of men. Was this the life she'd choose to escape to? She looked around at the other tables. Everyone seemed pleased with them-selves, happy with their life choices.

At least here, surrounded by dark wood and white tablecloths, nobody but Helen knew. In this city she could sit at her desk and look at the harbour and maybe she'd feel different, maybe she'd be able to forget the way he looked; his little body already cold. Maybe here she could forget this feeling.

'So, what does that handsome boyfriend of yours think about all this?' Helen said after they'd clinked glasses, after they'd ordered mains of fish in buttery sauces that Claire wasn't sure she'd be able to keep down.

'We haven't really had a chance to talk about it yet,' Claire said, the champagne like acid in her stomach.

Helen pulled a face that said, *Yikes* – her eyes wide, an eyebrow raised. 'Based on how you went today, you'd best put that on the agenda soon.'

'I just didn't want to bring it up in case there wasn't anything to bring up,' Claire explained, and was glad when a waiter in a white shirt and black waistcoat approached the table with two plates, distracting them.

As they ate, Helen ran through the list of Claire's classmates from her Environmental Law elective, seeking updates. Claire had been her favourite from day one, everyone knew it, but she still remembered the names of the others.

'Evelyn. Still a history teacher?' Helen asked.

Claire nodded, her mouth full of flaking white fish.

'They're lucky to have her.' Helen speared a new potato with her fork. 'Is Justin McPherson still a prick?'

Claire laughed.

Justin McPherson: the man with the widest face she'd ever seen. Al had only met him once and straight away googled the scene in *Drop Dead Fred* when Fred's face gets squashed in the fridge door. Claire had sent it to Ev, who'd passed it on, and before long everyone they knew was calling him Fred. He still didn't know why.

She'd never told Al that she'd had sex with Justin once in second year. If you could call it that. His pursuit of her had been relentless and one night she finally gave in. She'd told Ev about it the next morning – about how Justin couldn't get hard but had tried to squeeze his penis inside her anyway. 'This has never happened to me before,' he whimpered in the dark. She snuck out while he snored loudly, and he'd been rude to her ever since. Or, rather, he'd always been insufferable, but after that night it seemed more pointed, more direct.

'I assume so,' Claire said. 'We go to great lengths to avoid him.'

'Good,' Helen said. 'I never liked that entitled little shit.'

OUTSIDE THE RESTAURANT, Helen embraced her again, for longer this time. As if this time she was trying to seal the deal. She promised she'd be in touch, said not 'goodbye' but 'see you soon'.

Claire stood alone on the street corner. Streams of well-dressed, well-groomed workers passed her on the way to meetings, to and from lunch. It felt not unlike Melbourne on a busy day. This new life could be not unlike her old life. Just more humid, more free.

She looked at her phone. She had a while before she needed to leave for the airport. She hailed a cab and directed it to Bondi.

It wasn't until the taxi passed Centennial Park that Claire realised Helen hadn't asked about Nathan.

After it had happened, word spread through the alumni and professional whisper networks. She'd received four emails, two Facebook messages and a DM on LinkedIn asking for an address to send flowers to. She ignored them all and yet, days later, at Nathan and Annie's – she and Al there because they didn't know where else to go or what else to do – she noticed flowers and cards from everyone who'd contacted her. Claire wasn't sure what flowers were supposed to offer the bereaved. Nothing could ever fill the dark void Annie and Nathan would feel for the rest of their lives. Annie barely seemed to notice the flowers. Not when they were taking up every spare surface in the house, not when they were wilting, the water gone brown. All of them, everything, rotting and returning to the earth eventually. When Claire and Ev sorted through the bouquets and boxes, they made a pile of cards in case Nathan and Annie ever felt the need to say thank you.

'Surely people don't do this to be thanked afterwards?' Ev had asked as Claire folded a limp and browning bunch of lilies into the green bin by the side gate.

'Why does anyone do anything?' Claire had replied.

The question echoed through her head in the back of the taxi. Why was she here? What was she doing?

IT WAS HOT at the beach. There were near-naked bodies sprawled on towels on the sand, the ocean dotted with surfers, slick like seals in their black wetsuits. She walked down through the car park, took her shoes off at the top of the ramp, then made her way along the sand towards the waves. The water was cerulean, the water was the colour of her birthstone, the water was the colour of his lips. She'd thought it was a myth that lips turn blue but she saw it. She saw it vividly for days after. In bright flashes. Less often now, but the image hadn't faded completely. She tried to shake it from her mind as the waves churned the sand over and over and over.

She pulled out her phone and took a picture of the long curve of white beach, postcard perfect. She walked up the steps past the sandy change rooms and took a picture of Icebergs too, of white water smacking the edge of the ice-blue pools. She thought about sending it to someone. She thought about calling someone, telling them the plan she was putting into action. She searched back through her recent calls. Her finger hovered over her dad's number, over Ev's, over Al's. She locked her screen, put her phone away.

She took the steps back down to the beach and walked along the edge of the water. She imagined herself living here alone. She could get an apartment with a glimpse of the sea. Top floor, lots of light, floorboards. White walls, big windows and plants, and a balcony where Crunchie could sit and watch the world go by. She tried to imagine a life here with Al and tears welled in her eyes.

She knew she always did this. She moved. She ran away. She'd done it when her parents split up at the end of high school, applying only to universities that were as far away from Perth as possible. She'd done it to Ed. And she was doing it now. Running from her friends' grief, running from her own, running, most of all, from Al's before it swallowed them both.

A wave crashed a little closer than she expected and the tide rushed towards her, wetting her feet, the froth of the waves wetting the bottom of her trousers. She let it sweep in and out, let the next one come too and the next one.

Three

FOUR OF HEARTS ON FIVE of clubs.

'Finally,' Nathan whispered. It was the king of hearts he'd been waiting for.

He was eight games deep, maybe more. He was obsessed with trying to beat his best time of one minute and thirty-two seconds. Not obsessed – determined. Mesmerised by the monotony of it, by the simple logic.

On the other side of the bathroom door, the six staff members he employed were working very hard to keep the company running, taking meetings to woo new clients and appease the old ones. Those five lawyers and one assistant were the only reason he still had a company, still had a place to spend Friday afternoon putting one card on another on another on another. He'd tried to work. He'd sat at his desk and tried to answer some emails, he'd sat on calls with clients, sat in boardrooms and in coffee shops. He'd flown up to Canberra and not been able to leave his hotel room.

The problem was he couldn't think – not about work, not about anything. He couldn't force his brain to concentrate. It was as if there were a wall up in there. One of those plexiglass screens they have in prisons. He was the prisoner and the work was the visitor. No, the work was the prisoner and he wasn't allowed to touch it. Even the ins and outs of this bad analogy were too much for his brain to follow. For a year now, Nathan had felt as though his whole body was wrapped tightly in a bandage. As though the circulation had been cut to his limbs, to his brain, to his heart. As though his nerve endings were severed, his vision was impaired. Nathan had felt that he was, quite possibly, dead inside. One morning soon after it had happened, he'd woken in darkness, the blackout blinds drawn, and for a minute he thought that maybe he was dead on the outside too. That he was dead. That this liminal place, his life now, with its long empty hours, was purgatory. That this pain, this emptiness, hollowness, this boredom would last for an eternity.

He just needed a red jack to finish the game. The last game before he would go back to his desk. The problem with a small office, he'd remembered when he had been sitting on the toilet for close to twenty minutes, was that everyone would know he'd been sitting on the toilet for close to twenty minutes. Everyone knew that he, Nathan Woodward – one of Forbes' 40 under 40; political playmaker; man of influence; son of the great businessman Bob Woodward – had not done any real work for months. Almost a year to the day, actually.

He'd gone back to work too quickly. He knew, everyone knew, though no one said it because he was Nathan Woodward. But where else was he supposed to go? At work, they let him wallow. At work he had no one to look after but himself. No one said anything when he left meetings to sit in the toilets and cry. They just carried on like it was business as usual.

He wondered, let the thought creep in sometimes, whether this would've been easier if he was no one, if he was just some guy. It wouldn't have been written about in the paper. News wouldn't have spread around the neighbourhood, not to his favourite bottle shop nor the good bakery around the corner, not to the local pub.

There was one morning when he'd been awake since three (the sleeping pills hardly touched the sides by then) so he'd got up early to get bread. The three of them had gone to the bakery every Saturday. A coffee each for him and Annie, a cookie or a croissant for the kid. It was the first time he'd been into the shop since (it had been three weeks without him by then – how?), but as soon as he stepped through the door, he knew he'd made a mistake. He saw their eyes: so full of pity. He wanted to turn around and leave but it was too late.

'I'm so sorry,' one of the women said, flour streaked across her dark blue apron.

'A parent should never have to bury their child,' the barista chimed in.

A third person: 'I have two little ones of my own. I just can't imagine.'

Nathan wasn't sure exactly what happened next but he remembered yelling. No discernible words, just noises expelled at volume. And then he found himself in a nearby alley, where he threw a golden loaf of sourdough he couldn't remember paying for as hard as he could against the back wall of someone's house. It hit the bricks with a thud and then fell onto the slate-grey cobblestones. He went home without bread. He went home and cried on Annie's shoulder, unable to explain what he'd done, just how awful he felt.

They'd run out of words.

He'd walked past the loaf a few days later: its body had been hollowed out by pigeons, its crust soggy, soaked by rain. He'd never gone back to that bakery. He was too ashamed. Too worried about how they'd react to him now that he'd scorned their pity. The weeping bereaved are more forgivable than the angry bereaved.

Now when he needed bread he went to the supermarket or walked the extra two hundred metres to the bakery that wasn't as good. No wonder people were so scared of death, were terrified of its aftermath. The inconveniences it caused.

Nathan was just about to start a new game of solitaire when his phone rang, the vibration echoing off the bathroom tiles.

On the screen, it said: *Number 32.* A neighbour.

He let it go to voicemail, then waited for the message notification to pop up. He was sick of them. The neighbours. The way they dropped in to see if he and Annie needed anything. The way they glanced at the house as they walked by, shaking their heads at the tragedy of it all. He was sure that he'd seen their eyes scanning down Annie's body over the last few months, peering at her stomach to see if she was pregnant, looking for a bump. As if that would solve things.

He put his phone to his ear.

'Nathan, hi. Hi. It's Lydia from number thirty-two. Look, I don't want to alarm you, but I just walked past your place and I saw Annie in the yard doing, well doing some . . . gardening. It's none of my business, of course, but maybe you want to check in on her. Happy to pop over if you need. Okay, give me a call back if you want. Or not. No problem either way. Okay, from number thirty-two, Lydia.'

A sense of dread washed over him. What now? He tried to imagine the scene at home. Annie crying in the front garden. Annie standing in the front garden staring into space. Annie up a tree out the back threatening to jump. Annie with her insides scooped out, a hollow sack of skin. Annie a vacuum of all feelings. Annie a thin straight line. Annie a ghost in a white sheet. Annie a wisp. Annie gone too. Everything gone.

He knew he had to head home but he didn't want to.

He stood up, fastened his pants, flushed. He looked at himself in the mirror. His appearance still surprised him these days. How old he looked. How quickly it had happened. The dark circles forming under his eyes. The grey appearing in the tapered sides of his dark brown hair, before spreading quickly as though contagious. He'd lost weight. His belt notches proved it. That was from the stress at first. Now sometimes he'd just forget to eat. His fitness had suffered too. The muscles he'd built and sustained through decades of morning runs and twice-weekly gym sessions deteriorated quickly. He was withered. Weak. Men shouldn't be weak. That's what he'd been taught.

He washed his hands, put his phone in his pocket and skulked from the bathroom back to his office. If no one made eye contact, no one had to acknowledge how long he'd been in there. He sat at his desk, nudged his mouse, heard the ping of emails dropping into his inbox. He ignored them all and opened the solitaire app he'd downloaded on his desktop. As soon as he beat his best time, he'd go home. It would be a good omen.

There was a knock at the door and Nathan looked up to see Alex, his assistant, leaning against the doorframe, phone in hand. She reminded him a bit of Ev in the two short years she'd practised law: how she never looked comfortable in her office clothes, never seemed comfortable in that job.

'Am I pushing this call with the Minister for Immigration again?' Alex asked, as if she already knew the answer.

'No,' Nathan said so decisively it caught them both off guard. 'Let's do it.'

'Okay then.' Alex smiled as if she'd seen a hint of the old Nathan, as if maybe he was back. He could come back; he was sure he could. Alex turned on her heel. He saw her nodding to some colleagues, both of whom raised their eyebrows in surprise, as if to say, *This should be interesting*, or, *About time he did some work*.

He was sure they all talked behind his back. He knew they went to the pub together most Fridays to drink the week away, to complain about their useless boss.

He paused for a moment, tried to settle his thoughts. Then he picked up his phone to do what he always did: he called Ev.

Four

SHE WOULD NEVER SAY IT aloud, but Ev loved school the most when the kids had gone home, the classrooms empty of the stink of teenage boys, of the narrow-eyed sneer of fifteen-year-old girls. She loved the kids; she did. Most of them. Some of them. But the place felt hallowed when it was empty. Almost holy somehow.

Ev sat at her desk in the humanities office: a squat room, square, with so many desks crammed in so tightly that the chairs bashed into each other if two people stood up at the same time. There was an illustrated poster with Whales of the World on one wall, greasy at the corners with old Blu Tack. Ev had stared at it for long enough over the last five years that she knew most of them by heart. Sometimes, when she couldn't sleep, she'd picture her favourite whales – the big ones, weird ones. Always in the same order: blue, sperm, humpback, southern right, North

Atlantic right, narwhal, fin, bowhead, minke – their long wet bodies, their fins and flukes, barnacles crusted to their heads like the bows of ships.

On the desk in front of her was a pile of year ten history assignments, mostly marked. Only four to go. She could finish them before she left and have the evening free, the weekend free. She was lucky: her last two classes on Fridays were always free periods and so it had just gone three thirty and she'd finished almost all the work that would otherwise clog up her weekend. She shivered a little at the thought of this weekend, the hairs on the back of her neck standing on end. She reached for the cardigan she kept draped over the back of her chair, picked the curly black hairs from its shoulders, from its back, dropped them on the old blue carpet, then slipped it onto her shoulders.

Just four more assignments to mark.

'Hey,' Ev heard a voice say from the door. She looked up to see Queenie, head of her department, leaning against the door, her short, dark hair streaked with grey. 'I wanted to stop by and wish you well for tomorrow.'

Tomorrow.

'Thank you.' Ev sighed.

'Are you doing anything to commemorate?' A hint of Queenie's Filipino accent was still there even after twenty years away from home. She moved into the room, leaned against the edge of one of the geography teachers' desks, her long pink nails bright against the dark wood.

'No one's organised anything yet,' Ev said. 'Did you . . . do a thing?'

Queenie had cried when Ev told her what had happened. A week later it was Queenie who'd given her the name of the therapist Ev had been seeing every fortnight since. It was Queenie who gave her all the days off she needed (even some she didn't). Queenie's sister had lost her baby at eight months, had to labour as if she was giving birth to a live baby. Queenie had been her birth partner, had watched the little girl emerge lifeless into the world. Queenie even arranged a funeral, her sister unable to get out of bed. Queenie got it.

'Everything's different once you've seen behind the curtain,' she'd said, and Ev understood. She'd talked to the therapist about how grief and trauma can cast a shadow over everything. Things you don't expect. Things you won't even realise are in the dark because your eyes have adjusted.

'I went over, made her some food. I think I cleaned the house. Sometimes just showing up is enough.'

Queenie had a round face, a long neck, sunspots on her temples. Maybe it was just the influence of her name, but Ev had always thought of her as regal. The kids were terrified of her. Not because she was scary but because they liked her so much they didn't want to disappoint her. Ev felt the same.

'Thank you,' Ev said. 'I don't know if I could've got through the last year without you.' She meant it. Ev felt that Queenie had caught her as she was falling and carried her through the worst of it.

'We broken ones have got to stick together,' Queenie said with a wink. 'Text me tomorrow if you need anything. Or if you want Monday off. Leave me a voicemail if you just want to scream.'

Ev smiled, picturing Queenie with her phone held at arm's length as Ev screamed into the void.

'I'll be fine.' Ev nodded as if confirming this for herself. She looked down at her desk. 'Once I've marked these last few assignments, I'll be fine.'

'Who've you got left?' Queenie asked.

'Year ten: Kai Saunders and his little henchmen.'

'Oh, please read me a bit.' Queenie moved towards Ev's desk in anticipation.

Ev pulled Kai's paper from the pile.

'Okay, the assignment was: *Explain the factors that led to the development of the Nazi Party and the popularity of Hitler following World War I.*'

'An easy one,' Queenie observed.

'You'd think so,' Ev said. She started silently reading ahead. It was worse than she expected. She laughed in shock.

'Hit me, I'm ready.' Queenie rubbed her hands together with glee.

Ev cleared her throat: '*Women and women's rights were partly responsible for the rise of feminazis.*'

She could imagine Kai writing it then sniggering as he showed it to his mates. She threw it back down on the pile. These assessments were as much a test of her patience as they were of the kids' knowledge retention.

Queenie groaned.

'At least he spelled "responsible" correctly,' Ev said.

'He does have the best English teacher around.' Queenie pretended to dust off her shoulders. She headed for the door. 'Get those last ones done and get out of here.' She turned. 'And remember, if you need anything . . .'

'I know, thank you,' Ev said and Queenie was gone, her footsteps squeaking off down the lino-covered hallway.

Ev quickly marked the rest of Kai's assignment. It was only two paragraphs long, it didn't contain a single correct fact and, worst of all, he'd drawn a cock and balls at the bottom of the page in pencil and then rubbed it out. The impression was still there. It was enough to get him in big trouble again. There was no way he was going to pass, no way he could move on to year eleven. She wanted to be the teacher who'd get through to him, the teacher who made a difference. But she wasn't sure it was possible to help people who didn't want to be helped. She wrote, *Come see me after class, please*, at the bottom and left off his grade, which could only be a fail.

The other three weren't quite as bad. The handwriting of one was barely legible, but he'd tried. Another at least mentioned

World War I. The last just said: *With all due respect, Miss Greene, it happened two hundred years ago. I don't really care.*

She would've given him half a mark if he'd at least got the timing right.

Everything she tried to teach these kids in their history lessons was about consequences. A simple life lesson about how different the entire world could've been if just one little thing had changed. History showed you that the world was a centuries-long game of dominoes. All of it: prelude and aftermath. All of it: ghosts, memories, legacies left in its wake. Residue visible everywhere. The world was covered in the dust of the past.

Ev packed her laptop in her bag, followed by the Tupperware container that still had the dregs of her salad from lunch, a shred of lettuce drowning in dressing. Her diary, her wallet, keys, ID. Phone in her back pocket. She swapped the cardigan for her backpack, closed the office door behind her. Compared to her two years as a lawyer, where time was accounted for in six-minute increments, where phone calls were charged, where her every thought was billed and monetised, where every day she hoped it would get more interesting or more meaningful, being a teacher felt liberating. In the last year, it had felt life-saving.

The following week, year twelve exams would start, and soon she'd get to see her first batch of year sevens graduate. Gangly twelve-year-olds one minute, high school graduates the next. She'd been intimidated by the kids at first. Too worried about whether or not they'd like her, what names they'd call her behind her back. But she didn't think about that after she'd met them; after she'd started teaching them about all the cruelties and wonders of the world.

When she started out she'd been intimidated by the other teachers, too. Some of them were years younger than her – graduating from their three-year teaching degrees straight out of high school, up in front of their first classes before their twenty-second birthdays. But by the end of her first week she realised none of it mattered. No one cared what school she'd gone to, where she got her law degree, where she interned, how old she was, who she knew. They were just happy to have someone like her onboard. Someone who was curious, hungry to learn, someone who cared.

She retrieved her bike from the shed. Most of the bikes in there belonged to the male teachers, some of them costing, she was sure, at least a few months' salary. Matt-black frames, some so light she could lift them with a finger, others so heavy she worried they'd break something if they fell on her. Their owners would trot into the staffroom in the mornings in too-tight bike pants that revealed the outlines of things she found difficult to forget.

Ev's bike was a hand-me-down from her brother's now ex-girlfriend. Its gears clunked and rattled when she changed them, and the chain fell off about once a month, but it got her through the fifteen-minute ride between home and school. It got her down along the creek to Fitzroy North.

She put her helmet on, clipped it under her chin and pushed her bike to the back gate. She swung her leg over and was just about to start pedalling when she felt her phone vibrating in her back pocket.

She dug it out and looked at the screen: *Nathan Woodward*. The photo a close-up of his face, out of focus except the dark hollows of his nostrils, a big booger inside. It was from before. She hadn't replaced it. The memory of how things were was comforting sometimes.

'Hey,' she answered.

'Can you go to the house?' Nathan asked.

'I don't even get a hello anymore?' Ev said dryly, an attempt at humour.

'Sorry, Evelyn. Hello, can you please go to my house?' Nathan was much shorter with her these days. Shorter with everyone. He used to call just to say hi, to invite her over to dinner, to remind her of a funny thing that had happened a million years ago but had just popped into his head – he'd already be laughing when she answered. Now he only called to ask for things. And she'd answer. Every time.

'What's happening?' Ev asked.

'I'm not sure. One of the neighbours called and said that Annie's out in the garden.' He sighed. 'That's all I know.'

'Are you sure I'm the one who should go?' Ev was worried about what she'd find when she got there.

'I've got a meeting I can't miss,' Nathan said. 'I wouldn't ask if there was another way. Ev, please.' It wasn't said impatiently, but there was a tone to his voice that hinted at how he was feeling. The clipped tone of extreme sadness, depression, devastation, anger. An orchestra tuning up. The cacophony of grief.

'Okay,' she said. 'I'll go now.'

'I'll be home as soon as I can,' he said and hung up.

Ev put her phone back in her pocket and rode south along the slow moving, muddy creek. She dinged her bell at the walkers, at the runners who took up the whole path. She rode under the dappled shade of the long reaching arms of the white-trunked gums. She replayed Nathan's words in her head: *Annie's out in the garden.* What did that mean? She'd been trying to learn not to catastrophise. To remember that nothing was ever as bad as you thought it was going to be (except when it was). Ev pictured Annie sitting in the dirt crying, tears streaking her round freckled cheeks. Ev pictured Annie hanging from a branch of the crepe myrtle, her thin legs dangling.

From the bike path, she turned left down the alley that ran alongside Nathan and Annie's house. Their ridiculous house. The big backyard, white marble kitchen as if from a magazine, the living area, the light in the bedrooms, everything just exactly right, just perfect. She used to find its niceness embarrassing. Its adultness. Their togetherness. Their completeness. They were mostly the same age, but Ev felt miles behind her friends.

She thought, as she did more often than she liked, about Nathan and Annie's wedding. More than the times they'd been out to dinners she couldn't afford, more than when she'd found herself buying a round of drinks on her credit card, the wedding was the day that stuck in her head. The day that seemed to cement the divide between them. The have-somethings and the have-everythings.

●

'WHY ME?' EV whispered to Claire as she zipped up the back of her bridesmaid's dress, a big pink swirl. She was sweating already and it was not even nine thirty. 'It's not fair.'

She turned to look at herself in the mirror. She did not have the height to wear that much fabric, and she hated not wearing a proper bra; her boobs were threatening to tumble out at any moment. Knowing her luck, it'd be just as the bride and groom said I do.

She adjusted the flower crown that was pinned to her hair, which had been straightened with hot irons and braided too tight, and was now held in place with half a can of Elnett, so that it felt more like plywood than hair. She resembled a giant Christmas ham.

'You look' – Claire paused to choose her words carefully – 'lovely.' When she said 'lovely' her voice went up an octave. Ev glared at her. Claire was already dressed in her suit, perfectly tailored to fit her long body.

'It just doesn't seem fair that you get to be a groomsman – groomsperson,' she corrected herself before Claire could do it for her. Ev pulled the sinking love heart neckline up, adjusting herself inside it, then fluffed up the tulle, the chiffon hissing and shooshing as it rubbed against itself.

'Annie wanted you,' Claire said. 'And Annie Richards-soon-to-be-Woodward always get what she wants.' She smiled wryly. In every group decision (where to go on holiday, where to meet for dinner), Annie always got her way. 'Plus,' Claire added with a glint in her eye, 'this way you can stand opposite Fran at the altar and imagine what could've been.'

Ev turned to glare at her friend again, was about to tell her to shut up, when Annie interrupted.

'Claire bear,' she yelled from the other side of the room, where a team of women were attending to her – two on hair, one on make-up.

'Sorry,' Claire whispered to Ev, then yelled, 'Coming,' to the bride.

Ev took in the chaos of the room. There were bouquets of flowers everywhere; half-empty glasses of champagne; tiny, crust-less sandwiches and pastel-coloured macarons piled on delicate china. The bridesmaids had been given strict orders to make sure Sandy, the mother-of-the-bride, didn't drink too much, lest she get rowdy in the speeches and handsy on the dance floor, but Annie's sister was nowhere to be seen. Sandy, half-empty champagne glass in hand, plopped herself down next to Ev.

'Nothing makes you feel older than being the mother of the bride,' she said, taking a swig of champagne, her three-piece teal linen skirt suit already crumpled.

'Why don't we get you something to eat, Sandy,' Ev suggested. 'It's a long time before dinner.' She stacked a plate with little egg-and-cress sandwiches, their edges as dry as Ev's hair. She handed the plate to Sandy, helpfully taking away her champagne glass and necking the last of it as she turned around.

In the other corner of the room was Cherie Woodward, the two sides of her mouth entrenched so deeply in a frown they were almost at her chin. Cherie had looked at Ev with such disgust the first time they'd met. It was as if Cherie could smell the single mum, the state school, the scholarship on her. The fact that Cherie had caught her making out with Fran by the wheelie bins at Nathan's twenty-first didn't help. But Cherie's opinion of her never really bothered Ev. She just did what she always did, treated Cherie as she would anyone else, with what Claire had once called aggressive kindness.

Ev poured herself another glass of champagne and edged closer to Cherie.

'Can I get you anything, Mrs Woodward?' She pointed to the buffet of food on offer. 'A sandwich, a drink?'

'Evelyn, that dress does nothing for your figure, does it?' Cherie asked, ignoring Ev's offer. 'At least there's no chance you'll take any attention away from the bride.'

'Is it not the sole purpose of the bridesmaids to make the bride look better?' Ev asked, and she fetched Cherie a drink anyway, delivered it with a plate of food and a smile.

IT HAD SHOCKED no one when Nathan told his friends he was going to propose to Annie. If anything, they were surprised it hadn't happened sooner. They'd been together more than a decade. There was never a question it was going to be any other way.

Ev had gone with Nathan to pick up the ring and laughed a little too hard when the sales attendants congratulated them on their engagement. Nathan knew what he wanted (Annie had been hinting for years) and he'd had it designed especially. Ev perused the shelves of the jewellery store. To her all the rings looked the same: big, expensive and out of reach. She watched as they rang up the sale at the till, as Nathan swiped his card without baulking: the total price a quarter of Ev's yearly salary. She wondered how different her life would be if she'd kept practising law. She'd be able to afford some of the nice things Nathan could, some of the nice things Claire could. But she'd still be miserable.

'Annie's going to love it,' Ev had said as they were let out of the store by a security guard. 'And if she doesn't, can I please have it to pay my rent?'

Nathan slowed his pace; his long strides usually had Ev chasing after him on the street.

'You know that if you're ever struggling I can help out,' he said. 'You only need to ask. In fact, you don't even need to ask. I'll just put some money in your account.'

'No way,' Ev said. 'I don't want your dirty money.' She pushed open the door to a wine bar that always seemed to be dark, even in the middle of the day. 'You can buy the drinks, though.'

EVEN THOUGH NATHAN was a staunch atheist and Annie only referred to herself as vaguely spiritual (and only after a good yoga class), the church ceremony was long, their vows sandwiched between Bible readings and hymns. When the priest said, 'Let us pray,' Ev looked around to see who really was praying. She looked past Annie's sister, past Annie, to Nathan, who stood with his eyes firmly shut. She wondered what he was thinking, if he was nervous or as sure of himself in this as he was in everything else in his life. Next to him was Fran, her brown hair thick like Nathan's, styled to accentuate its natural wave. She looked good in her suit, Ev thought. The thing between them, whatever it was, never got off the ground. A few drunken kisses, eager hands. Nathan wasn't against it exactly, but he wasn't supportive.

'It's my sister,' he'd said, his whole body cringing.

'I'm someone's sister,' Annie had pointed out.

'YOU NEVER SEE brides with colds,' Claire said later as she cut into her steak, a little drop of blood from its red centre splashing onto the tablecloth.

'The colds come on the honeymoon,' Ev said through a mouthful of chicken she'd stolen from Al's plate. The conversation at his table had bored him so much he'd dragged his chair over to theirs. 'When you let yourself relax into wedded bliss. A little reminder that no one's infallible.'

'I don't know,' Al said, moving his plate out of Ev's reach. 'These two are pretty perfect.'

The three of them watched Annie and Nathan shaking hands and kissing cheeks, pausing every so often to look at each other and smile.

They looked good together, Ev thought. They both looked just plain good. Annie in that dress. A few days after she'd shown Ev a picture of it, Ev had met Claire for dinner and they'd spent twenty minutes on Google trying to work out how much it cost. They found it, then had to put the phone face down on the table and breathe deeply to recover.

Good, scary smart, quick to laugh, loyal Claire. It might be all the champagne, but Ev teared up looking at her. She loved her. Loved Claire's enormous boyfriend, too.

From her spot at the head table, Ev was able to survey the room for potential suitors. There was a table of men from Nathan's posh boys' school. Most of them were married to women who still played hockey. Although the men were the same age as her, they all seemed to have aged faster – as if their bodies grew tired from being so intolerably boring. She cast an eye over Annie's side of the family. No cute cousins, no secretly gay schoolfriends, no one who didn't seem to already be partnered up.

There were two tables of grey-haired, buttoned-up lobbyists and former politicians. Unfuckable. These were men Bob Woodward kept in his pocket for favours. Men she knew Nathan hated for their enduring presence throughout his life: loitering in groups at family birthday parties and barbecues. ('What's the collective noun for a group of politicians?' Nathan had whispered to her when they'd shown up at his graduation party. 'A lie?' Ev had suggested. 'No, an impotence,' she added, and Nathan laughed so hard beer almost came out of his nose.) The few Ev recognised were responsible for some of the state and country's worst decisions: funnelling money away from people with disabilities, locking up asylum seekers. Just the sight of them made her sick. They were more than a lie; they were criminals. She wished gout upon them all.

The worst of them clinked a knife on the side of his glass and stood to make his father-of-the-groom speech. She'd promised Nathan that she'd behave herself tonight, keep her politics off the table, but it wasn't that easy. Here she sat with access to some of the country's most powerful men. How often did anyone get that kind of opportunity? She wanted to have three whiskies and then corner each one of them and give them a piece of her mind, tell them what they could have done better, what they could still be doing better. But of course she wouldn't. Because Nathan had asked her not to? Or because she was a coward? She liked to think it was the former but would always know, deep down, that it was the latter. Nathan would forgive her.

She looked at her lap for much of Bob's speech, worried people would notice the grimace on her face. But when he made a joke about marriage equality – 'These days, you're allowed to marry anyone or anything; we're glad our son chose Annie, not a dog or a bridge,' his whole body shaking as he chuckled at his own joke – Ev's gaze moved to Fran, who kept her eyes fixed on Tess. Ev knew Nathan had battled with Cherie to ensure Tess and her daughter Ruby had a seat at the front of the room with the rest of his family. Ruby sat between her mothers in her flower girl dress, overstimulated, tired, fidgeting with the pink and white roses pinned in her hair.

Behind Fran was a table full of their other uni friends. Al, relegated back to his seat among them for the speeches, was a fish out of water. He caught her eye and she laughed as he scratched his nose so that his middle finger was subtly extended to her. She brushed a fallen strand of hair from her face with her own, smiled. The secret language of friends.

LATER, AFTER SHE'D cried through the first dance, Ev stood at the edge of the dance floor, nursing a red wine, and watched Al and

Claire together. He was moving with such vigour he'd busted two buttons from his shirt. He was about a foot taller than everyone else; that and his big wedge of black hair meant people would sometimes stare. She often saw him trying to make himself smaller in public, slouched or crouching to fit in better. On the dance floor, five drinks in, he didn't care. Claire cried laughing as he jutted his hips in time to the music, jumped around in small circles. As much as Ev tried to fight it, as much as she wanted to be okay, to be strong and independent, moments like this seeped into the cracks and she found herself jealous, sad, wanting.

She prowled around the edge of the dance floor, weaving in and out of groups of men laughing loudly, groups of men drinking together, groups of men who preferred the company of each other to their wives and girlfriends, who were dancing to Rhianna or making idle chitchat with each other on the sidelines.

Ev was drunk. Her ridiculous skirt brushed the legs of people as she passed them. Her feet hummed: her arches sore, her toes cramped, her heels rubbed raw. Annie had made her promise she wouldn't take the too-high heels off until she was on her way home. ('It's uncouth to be barefoot at a wedding,' Annie had said, repeating a scolding she'd apparently received from Cherie once. Ev couldn't help but laugh at her. Annie crossed her arms and pretended to sulk.)

Ev found a spot at the back of the room, a stray chair near the door. She collapsed into it, kicked off her shoes, lifted her foot to rest it on her knee and looked at the blister that had formed on the side of her big toe. She'd read once that the liquid in blisters gathers to cushion the tissue underneath, to protect it from further damage. She touched it lightly. It reminded her of a waterbed. She rubbed the sole of her foot with her thumbs. She swapped legs, needled fingers into pressure points. There was some blood on the inside of one of her shoes. There was no way she could put them back on.

In the flashing lights, the glitter pedicure on her toes sparkled. All the primping and preening felt ridiculous, pointless. The mental tally of the money she'd spent on this wedding made her feel anxious: the hen's weekend, the mixed-bucks party for Nathan, the engagement present and wedding present, a pedicure, a manicure. She didn't earn what the others did, and every outlay stung a little. Every outlay meant she'd have to scrimp on something else. But it was nothing compared to the cost of the wedding itself. The venue, the flowers on every table and on every pew in the church. All that champagne, the exquisite food. Thinking of the food, her stomach rumbled so loudly she feared it might be audible over 'Rock Lobster', now pumping out of the speakers to an appreciative dance floor. She wondered what had happened to the leftover cake. Collecting her shoes in one hand, she went searching.

A long hall ran from the reception room to the rest of the hotel with big glass doors leading to the gardens. Smokers stood in small clumps, puffing white smoke into the warm night air. Against one wall, a couple were making out. Him pressed against her, his hands on her hips, on her back, lower. Ev felt a single throb between her legs. There was nothing like the celebration of other people's love to make you feel the sharp absence of it in your own life, a familiar mix of being alone and horny. She hobbled along the parquet floor.

On the other side of the hall were doors leading to various other conference and event rooms and, finally, to the kitchen. Ev pushed the door open a little and peered inside. What was left of the bottom tier of the cake was being cut into slices and put into little white takeaway boxes. The top tier stayed intact, the mini Annie and Nathan that Ev'd had specially made by someone she'd found on Etsy stood proud atop their white-iced wonderland. Ev slipped through the door and stood at the table where the already-boxed slices were being stacked. One of the kitchen staff passed her a box with a wink. She opened it, stuck her finger into the icing, licked it off. Closing the lid, she smiled sweetly and swiped a second box.

Out in the hallway, she looked for a quiet spot to sit and eat – a nook, an unused room, a sofa. She turned a corner and near the cloakroom saw Nathan, hands in the pockets of his Tom Ford suit, Annie next to him. They were talking to Bob and Cherie.

Ev looked on as Bob handed Nathan an envelope. He looked at it with mock suspicion. Annie watched him intently as he opened it and pulled out a cheque. Ev couldn't see the amount written on it but she heard Annie gasp.

'It's too generous,' Nathan said. 'We couldn't possibly.'

'It's enough to get you into a house with room for a family,' Bob said, and Nathan shook his hand, thanked him. Annie jumped up and down and thanked them twice, three times. She hugged both of them. In a rare show of affection, Cherie actually returned the embrace. Nathan kissed his mother's cheek, folded the cheque and slid it into the inside pocket of his suit jacket. To Ev, they looked as though they were bathed in golden light. A combination of wealth and happiness. All straight, glinting teeth and loose shoulders. Good breeding, good dentistry.

Ev stepped back and paused so she'd remember this moment through the haze of her drunkenness, her exhaustion. Then she took her two boxes of cake and went back up the hall and through the door into the garden. On a sandstone bench near a jumble of sweet lavender, she dumped her shoes, sat cross-legged and opened one of the boxes of cake, the cardboard already stained with grease from the buttery icing. Behind her a man laughed loudly, a woman giggled. She pulled off a chunk from the outside of the cake: delicate sponge, sugary icing, the tartness of the lemon curd, a hint of elderflower. It was delicious; truly otherworldly delicious. She closed her eyes as she chewed and swallowed. She pulled off another chunk and another and another, opened the second box and polished that off too. It felt good to give in to desires, to savour. She stacked the boxes on the seat next to her and let herself imagine what she'd do with the money if someone handed her a cheque. She'd buy a house. Nothing extravagant. A two-bedroom unit or a little cottage near her rental in Brunswick East with enough space out the back to eat outside, to grow vegetables. She'd fly to London, get the train north, walk some of Hadrian's Wall; cross the Channel to Normandy and try to commit every stitch of the Bayeux Tapestry to memory. Back at school, she'd describe it all to the kids, help them to see it too.

Ev had grown up understanding that money was something that didn't come easily. That it was a thing to be worried about. That what she ate and how much, that how she dressed, that following trends, being cool, maintaining friendships were all dependent on having it. She got a job as soon as she could. Stacking shelves at the supermarket first, then working the register. And she'd never not worked since. Even with a partial scholarship for her law degree (more money than her mum had ever seen in one lump sum), she could never rest. And now she knew she'd be paying off the rest of her law degree and her Master of Teaching for at least another few years. She didn't own a house or a car, and she hadn't travelled much. But she was lucky. She knew that. She had a good job and food and clothes and a roof over her head and friends she loved, her health. She knew she was lucky. But just once, she let herself think, just once she wanted to be given something without having to work for it, without it feeling hard. Just once.

'There you are,' Claire said as she walked into the garden holding three takeaway boxes of cake. Ev hastily pushed her two boxes onto the ground, kicking them under the bench to hide them. Al was behind Claire, in his hands three crystal glasses, each containing a double shot of whisky. Claire sat on one side of her, Al on the other, and they shared out the cake and whisky between them.

'To love,' Claire said, her glass held aloft. They clinked their drinks together. As Ev tucked into her fourth piece of cake for the evening, washing it down with expensive alcohol purchased on someone else's dime, sandwiched between her two friends in a beautiful garden, she really did feel lucky. She did. She did. She did.

•

SHE PULLED UP at the corner, the brakes of her bike squeaking, and over the picket fence saw Annie on her knees in the front garden. Around her, every native plant she and Nathan had meticulously chosen – or the landscape architect had chosen – had been pulled up by the roots. The long silvery branches of the silver princess had been hacked with an axe and were strewn across the yard. The whole thing was ruined.

'Annie,' Ev whispered from the other side of the fence as she watched Annie tug at the grevillea, its flowers the gradient of a sunset from pink to yellow. 'What have you done?'

She took the lock from her backpack and linked it through the strap of her helmet, through the bike, attaching both to the fence. She walked slowly around to the front gate, wondered when or if Annie was going to notice she was there. She saw Annie stand and pick up the axe.

The gate creaked as she opened it. Annie gasped, dropped the axe at her feet.

'Ev!'

'Nath asked me to come over and' – Ev wanted to say: *see if you've really lost it this time* – 'see you. So what's going on?' she asked lightly, as if there was nothing alarming about the destruction of a garden.

'I'm gardening,' Annie said. There was dirt caked under her fingernails, all over her clothes, a twig caught in the loose curls of her blonde hair.

Ev looked around at the mess. There were unearthed kangaroo paws, native grasses with their roots exposed, holes where they used to be.

'I don't know if it counts as gardening if you've just pulled everything up.' Ev stood with her hands on her hips. Maybe they could just stick it all back in the ground, water it, hope the roots would take hold again. She got down on her knees next to Annie and picked up a bush of pink native daisies, dirt hanging from its roots. 'We can probably just replant it.'

'I don't want to just replant it.' Annie snatched the bush from Ev and threw it on the ground with the others, then dropped back down to her knees.

'Annie,' Ev said patiently.

'It wasn't right,' Annie said, her hair falling over her face as she bent over to dig up a tuft of native grass. 'It's not right,' she whispered as she yanked the tuft from the ground.

Ev inched closer to her. 'Why don't we just stop for a bit?' she suggested gently. 'Take a break, have a cup of tea, then maybe I can help you sort this out.' She'd seen Annie in a variety of different states over the last year but never like this. This was new.

'I want to finish before he gets home. I want him to see.'

'See what?'

'I don't know, Ev. Just let me do this. I need to do this.' Annie was crying now, tears streaming through the dirt on her cheeks, cracked earth after rain. 'I went for a walk before,' she said. 'I was feeling okay so I went for a walk, and I walked past this house down the street and they had this big overgrown front yard. There were raised beds and vegetables and flowers spilling from them, and there were toys everywhere, and I heard the kids playing and shouting and I thought' – she dropped the grass onto the growing mound of dying plants – 'I thought that maybe if our garden was like theirs, messier or something . . .' Annie wiped her face with the back of her hand, dirt becoming mud.

'Then?' Ev said.

'What?' Annie looked at her. Ev had never seen anyone look so defeated.

'You were saying that if your garden was messy . . .' Ev thought she knew what was coming next, but she wanted Annie to hear how crazy it sounded.

'Then maybe he wouldn't have died.' Annie put her face in her hands and sobbed. 'Oh my god,' she gasped, raising her head and looking around at what she'd done. 'Nath's going to kill me.'

'He's not,' Ev said. She held out her arms and Annie collapsed into them; her hair smelled as though she hadn't washed it in a while. 'It was some flawed logic, but he'll understand.' She felt Annie's tears wetting her shoulder through her shirt. 'I always thought this garden was a bit wanky anyway,' she whispered.

Annie let out a snort and pulled back. 'Did you really think it was wanky?' She smiled through her tears, eyes glassy blue like the sea after a storm.

'Maybe a little. I mean, the whole house . . .' Ev gestured to the perfect home behind her.

'Hey.' Annie whacked Ev on the thigh with the back of her hand.

'Maybe we should just tear the whole thing down before your husband gets home, start again?'

'Oh my god, stop it.' Annie was no longer crying, at least, Ev was relieved to note. But what was she going to do with this mess?

'Wait, what are you doing here?' Annie eyed her suspiciously.

'One of the neighbours called Nath and he called me.'

Annie nodded slowly.

'Come on.' Ev stood and held her hands out to pull Annie up. Ev put her arm around Annie's shoulders as the two of them surveyed the damage. 'You get in the shower and I'll tidy up a bit.'

Annie stood quietly for a minute as if she might argue, or offer to help. Then she turned and went inside, letting the front door slam behind her.

Five

CLAIRE TOOK A CAB FROM the airport to the office; a twenty-five minute run just before school pick-up traffic clogged the roads. On the plane, she'd stared out the window watching the trees and buildings shrink and shrink until they looked like architectural models, the little cars zooming around on the roads like ants. Then it was just white clouds, it was just blue sky. It was just Claire alone with a future she was trying to re-shape, to re-imagine. In the past, she and Al had talked about travel, they'd talked about buying a house, even about kids. Lately, they'd barely talked at all. Can silence change the shape of things? All that air casting a secret spell.

Her rich lunch sat heavy as she took the lift up and up to the fifty second floor. She stared at her phone as she walked through the open-plan office, flicking mindlessly through her apps just to look busy, to feel busy. She noticed a little red dot on the Gmail envelope icon, the number one. A new email. It was probably a newsletter she'd accidentally signed up to when she bought something online and forgot to opt out of marketing emails. If only opting out were really an option, Claire thought.

The red dot seemed to hum, pulsate. A siren. Urgent.

It could be a shipping notification from the online shop where she bought Crunchie's cat food. An electricity bill. A water bill. Something from the bank. An invite to some alumni drinks; she hadn't had one of those for a while.

It wasn't, though. Claire knew somehow that it wasn't. She sat at her desk, turning her phone face down as if that would erase the little red dot, the number one from her mind. As if anything was that easy to forget.

She swivelled her office chair around and looked out the window. At layers of glass and metal that towered into the sky around her. She leaned over, resting her head against the window. The second day after moving from her desk in the open-plan area to this glass-walled office, she'd discovered that if she looked at just the right angle, she could see people walking on the street. Whenever she felt she needed perspective, she'd press her head against the glass and look down on their lives.

She took a deep breath. Another. Then she sat back, turned around, picked up her phone, unlocked it. It was from Helen.

The subject of the email: *Looking good.*

Under it, a preview of the email: *Team's on board. Just got to run it up the ladder.*

'Fuck,' Claire said and turned her phone face down.

She logged into her computer and turned her attention to her work email, looked at her list of things to do. It was long but not insurmountable. If there was one thing she was good at, it was getting on with things, it was getting the job done. Ev once told her she was good at compartmentalising, which Claire took as a compliment although she wasn't sure it was meant as one.

She hadn't spoken to Ev in a while. It wasn't that she was avoiding her. It was just that she was sure the minute she saw her, Ev would know. She would know about Sydney, she would intuit every one of Claire's thoughts and feelings, her worries and hurts, just as she always did. A sixth sense, a superpower. It was what made her such a good teacher, such a good friend, such an indomitable force walking through the world.

Claire remembered the first time she saw Ev, sitting in the second row of their first-ever Crim and Torts lecture.

Claire was seventeen, in a new city. She had a cousin in Melbourne, she'd kept in touch with a friend who'd moved over in year eight, and she was living in a share house with too many people, but she was ostensibly alone. She'd always been good at working, been good at school, but never good at friendships. Having laser focus, ambition and excelling at compartmentalising weren't qualities people often looked for in friends. But then there was Ev: wild dark hair, big brown eyes, about a foot shorter than Claire but with twice as much presence. Claire had never believed in love at first sight, but she saw Ev and almost ran to the seat beside her, put her books down, smiled awkwardly. Ev was already chatting to the guy on her other side: conventionally handsome, clean-shaven, neat brown hair – he looked like he'd come straight out of private school. He smiled at Claire, and that was that: she, Ev and Nathan were inseparable. Then they met Nathan's girlfriend, Annie, and it was as if a foundation had been laid.

They'd hang out at Nathan and Annie's to study together (their house was the nicest – Nathan's parents paid the rent). Annie would make them dinner, her assignments for her marketing major never taking as long as theirs. Claire suspected it had nothing to do with a law degree being harder, and everything to do with Annie being the smartest of all of them, the most determined, the most sure of what she wanted. She already had a job lined up as a marketing assistant at a schoolfriend's family's vitamin company. Like Nathan, everything had always fallen into place for her.

The few times Claire had seen Annie in the last few months, she'd noticed that she moved in a new way. As if her body were heavier, waterlogged. Claire picked up her phone, opened Annie's Instagram profile. She hadn't posted a picture in a year. Before that, there were daily updates: at the park; at home; the five of them together down at the beach, Al holding the toddler up so high in the air. It wasn't like Annie was living two different lives but like she was two different people. Like all signs of life had been zapped out of her. Claire had never experienced a pain as sharp as Annie's. She tried to imagine how it would feel. As though part of her was missing? As though she'd been cut open? How could Annie ever come back from this? Claire felt guilty for being unable to protect her, powerless to help her.

Claire closed Instagram, put her phone down, went back to her list, ignored her Gmail, ignored the feelings inside her, the niggling in her stomach, the ache in her jaw, ignored it all and did what she did best: locked it in a drawer and went back to work.

Six

EIGHT OF SPADES, THE SEVEN of diamonds next. From there it was easy to finish the game. It was easy to win. Nathan watched the cards fly around the screen of his phone. Success. He had won again. It was the fourth game he'd played in a row, sitting there in the front seat of his car a few doors up from his house. Just one more, he thought, and then he'd go in and face the music. Just one more and he'd find out what Annie had done. New game. Two aces on the draw boded well. He moved the cards around, his head so full of numbers there wasn't room for much else. His phone lit up, vibrated. He had her name saved as *Mother* for a while, but Annie made him change it. ('It's too cold,' she'd argued. 'Exactly . . .' he'd countered.) Now, *Cherie Woodward* flashed urgently.

He let it ring a few times then answered, knowing she'd never leave a message or send a text. It was always easier to dispense of Cherie quickly, politely. Any small slight was like a drop of water on sandstone to her. Enough of them and cracks would form, a crevasse, a landslide, houses tumbling from a cliff into the ocean.

'Nathan Woodward,' he said as if he didn't know it was her. He couldn't bring himself to say, *Hi, Mum*.

'Nathan, it's Cherie.' Her voice was stiff as ever.

'Hey, I'm just in the middle of something.' He wasn't lying. He had a queen and a jack sitting there, ready to go. The seconds he'd lose stopping and starting would make a difference to his time.

'I'm calling to confirm dinner tonight.' Cherie didn't give an inch.

'Yes, I remember.' He scrunched up his face. He hadn't remembered.

'Come at six thirty. Don't bring anything.' She always said this, but the few times they'd turned up empty-handed, her eyes had darkened, her lips had tightened.

He wondered what would happen if they didn't show up at all. He pictured Bob and Cherie sitting at the dinner table waiting for them. Waiting while the food went cold. Waiting while the gravy formed a skin, waiting while the bread dried out. He was sure they'd die there, just to make a point: Martha, the housekeeper, finding them already in a state of decay. The food between them rock-hard, covered in mould like lichen on rock, their flesh dripping off them while they pooled onto the Hans Wegner dining chairs. The room droning with flies.

'Okay, see you later.' He hung up, knowing there wouldn't be any warmth offered. Not a 'can't wait' or a 'looking forward to it'. Not in a million years. Nathan put his phone down in his lap.

'Shit,' he whispered.

Two bad phone calls in one day. Three if you counted the meeting he should've postponed again: a dressing-down from a federal minister about solutions promised but not delivered.

Nathan moved the ace of hearts, the two, the three. The whole game opened up and within thirty seconds he was done. He'd won. He was a grown man sitting in his car celebrating a solitaire win. He took a deep breath. Let it out. Took another. He could see the house from the driver's seat.

Nathan had spent months wondering if they should have moved after it happened. If the house was haunted, cursed. He knew it freaked people out, that they were reluctant to come over. And when they did, they'd walk from room to room casting their eyes around for evidence of where he'd died. Nathan had considered announcing it or drawing a chalk outline to save them the trouble.

The night – or rather morning; it had become morning without them realising – they came home from the hospital without him, Nathan felt both love and hatred for every room in the house. Their son was everywhere and nowhere at the same time. The only proof of life they had was a sticky handprint, a wayward sock, a drawing, a brush tangled with strands of his curly brown hair. It wasn't enough. It wasn't anywhere near enough.

Nathan undid his seatbelt slowly. He coached himself as he would before big meetings. *Come on, big guy, out of the car, let's see what we're dealing with.* He wiped the sweat from his top lip, from his forehead. It was not summer yet, but it was hot. One of those days where the air is clear but the breeze brings the threat of smoke and ash, of danger.

He approached the front gate and inspected the mess. The garden was destroyed. The small gum split through its trunk. There were piles of plants, holes where they'd been pulled up from their roots. Woodchips were scattered across the path. It looked like a tornado had hit, like an act of eco-terrorism. He wasn't sure how he was supposed to feel. Angry? Sad? Glad that Annie had done something, even if what she'd done was messy, destructive, hysterical? He didn't feel angry. He felt nothing.

He remembered back when they'd had the front garden redone. Annie had spearheaded the project, researching all the best native plants for the type of soil they had, working with a landscape architect, making cups of tea for the team who did the planting, sticking meticulously to the plan that Annie had approved down to the inch. All while seven months pregnant. She wanted the garden done for when their boy arrived (he was going to be called Benjamin then, maybe Andrew; would things have been different if they'd called him Andrew?), as if the two were connected somehow. She was always looking for links in things, always believed they happened for a reason. Until a year ago, that is, when they learned it was possible for the universe to just tear open for no reason.

He stepped over a pile of grasses, of dirt, let himself in through the front door. Upstairs, the shower was on. He walked down the hall, held his breath as he passed the kitchen, as he always did.

Ev was sitting on the wide green sofa, a beer in one hand, her phone in the other. She hadn't heard him come in, so he stood and watched her for a few seconds. She had her legs curled under her, her school clothes more sensible than her normal clothes.

'Oi,' Ev said. She'd caught him staring. 'What are you looking at?'

'Nothing,' he said, holding his breath as he walked back into the kitchen, past where it happened. Nathan didn't need a chalk outline to know the exact spot. His body would never forget. At the fridge, he drank straight from the SodaStream bottle. The water felt good. He was so thirsty. Always so thirsty. He slid a beer from the shelf and sat down beside Ev, took a few sips.

'So,' Ev said, breaking the silence, 'what did you think of the garden? It's a new landscaping trend apparently: natural minimalism, big on dirt. Low on maintenance. It'll be all over *Gardening Australia* before you know it.'

He knew what she was doing. It was what she'd always done: try to get a laugh out of him to ease the tension, as if that would fix things. He was too tired to laugh.

'Come on,' Ev pleaded. 'Give me something.'

'Sorry.' Nathan looked at her: the top part of her hair flat from her helmet, the rest curly, wild. 'I'm tired,' he said.

'I know.' She shifted on the sofa to face him.

'She's' – she swallowed loudly – 'she's just still so sad.'

'I know,' he said. 'Remember how she used to be?'

'Abnormally happy,' Ev said with smile.

'It was a bit sick, wasn't it?' Nathan smiled too. Annie would always see the bright side, always find a way to spin things. Sometimes he found it oppressive. Mostly he needed it. 'Are we supposed to do something?' he asked. 'Tomorrow, I mean.'

'I was going to ask about that.' She paused. 'Probably. But only if you want to. Do you want to?'

'I don't know,' he said. He knew he didn't want to sit around and listen to more empty platitudes from well-meaning people.

'Maybe it'd be good for Annie, help her move on.'

'Help her hurry up and get over it?' Nathan snapped. He sounded meaner than he'd meant to. He wanted that too, but he hated other people thinking it. Hated wondering about what they must think of her.

'You know that's not what I mean.' Ev sat back, folded her arms defensively. He knew she didn't think that, but there were others who did. His mother, who'd asked more than once when they were going to start trying again. As if his son was like a broken dish: replaceable.

'Oh god,' Nathan said, remembering the dinner at Bob and Cherie's. An anniversary dinner? he wondered. More likely thoughtless timing. 'We have to go to dinner in Toorak tonight.'

Ev pulled a face as if she'd smelled a fart.

'You could always just say no,' she said, and Nathan glanced at her from the corner of his eye. It didn't work that way and Ev knew it.

'So tomorrow,' Ev said, moving the conversation on. 'I can organise something, if you want. It could just be the five of us. Maybe we'd have fun?'

Nathan looked at her, said nothing.

'Just think about it,' Ev said, and Nathan nodded.

They sat quietly drinking their beers for a few minutes. Outside, the ding of the 11 tram, its wheels scuttling along the metal tracks. Outside, the wattle birds squawked and squabbled in the trees. Outside, the world carried on as normal, as though nothing was wrong, as though he wasn't dead, he wasn't gone.

'Did you know . . .' Nathan began. It was a thought that had plagued him in the last year.

Ev didn't probe, didn't rush him, gave him space to speak.

'That when we were seventeen . . .' He didn't know where to start. Didn't know how to talk about it. 'Annie got pregnant.'

'Yes,' Ev said calmly.

'She told you?' He couldn't imagine a time when it would've come up.

'Women talk about things,' Ev said. 'Remember in second year I was dating that real idiot?'

Which one? Nathan thought. There'd been a lot of them over the years. Mean-spirited men, boring men, a woman with dreadlocks whose name was something like Leaf or Branch. None of them good enough for her.

'Marcus with the . . .' She made a juggling motion down by her knees and it came flooding back to him. Marcus with the long balls. How could he forget? He nodded, and she continued.

'My period was late – Annie told me about her abortion to make me feel better.'

'Just like that?' He was often shocked by just how much of their bodies women shared with one another, how it bonded them.

'It's what we do,' she said, and he nodded, not really under-standing. He remembered once Annie had told him that everything men fear women talked about was true. And then some.

'Do you think she regrets it?' he asked.

'I don't think that's a thought either of you should be enter-taining right now,' Ev said firmly. 'It's not going to help anyone.'

'I know.' He took a sip of his beer and shifted his focus to the window. He didn't feel better for mentioning it. 'I've spent a year joining dots that aren't really there.'

Ev lifted herself on her knees so she could wrap her arms around his shoulders from the side. Nathan let her. He rested his head against her shoulder blade for a second; her thick curls fell like a curtain around both of them. He wanted to cry but he didn't let himself. He was sick of crying. Ev rubbed one hand in circles on his back and he let her go through the motions of soothing him.

'Annie dug up the garden because she thought maybe if the garden was different . . . he wouldn't have died. Or he'd come back,' Ev said.

'Christ,' he said, pulling back to look at her.

'It's like you're both walking in circles on different paths in the same forest,' she said.

He breathed, steadied himself.

They let it go quiet between them.

'I don't know what to do with her,' he said, on the verge of tears. 'I don't know what she's thinking. I don't know what she's feeling. I don't know how to fix it.'

'What does she say when you ask her?' Ev sat back down on her haunches, facing him.

'She shrugs, she cries, she gets frustrated with me, with herself.'

'And what about the therapist?'

'She stopped going. Said she didn't like her, that she didn't help.' He shook his head. 'I just want to make it better for her. I just want him not to have died.'

They sat and drank their beers quietly.

'Thank you for being here,' Nathan said finally.

'Always,' Ev said and smiled. He watched her drink the rest of her beer quickly. She put the bottle on the table and stood. 'But now I'm going to leave you to talk to your wife. Think about tomorrow, okay?' She placed her palms on his cheeks. Her hands were wet from the condensation on the bottle. 'I love you. You can do this.' She kissed him on the forehead, and he watched her collect her bag, swing it onto her shoulder and leave.

The front door closed, the house went quiet. A year ago, the house had been full of life, of noise, of love. Now, there were long stretches of silence that settled between he and Annie like a fog so dense it made it hard to see a way out, made it hard for them to see each other. Nathan felt like he was losing sight of the only thing he'd ever truly been certain about.

•

THERE'D BEEN GIRLS before her. There were weekend parties. They'd rotate between houses, choosing the ones big enough for them to hide away in a separate wing or where the parents were out at some function or other, either not caring what their kids got up to or turning a blind eye. They'd drink and watch music videos on *Rage*. Scott Reynolds often had a bit of weed on him and sometimes they'd do cones, smoke a joint, once they made a bong out of an old Coke bottle. It was fun. He always had fun. There was always a girl interested in him, too, one who'd let him put a hand up her top, in her bra, sometimes down the waistband of her jeans or up her skirt. His mates would all talk about it after – who got to do what to whom. But one thing Nathan never revealed was how he felt like he deserved all the things he got, that this was just how life was supposed to be. Would always be.

It wasn't until he met Annie that he realised something was missing. She arrived the first day of year eleven like sunshine after a cloudy day. There was a warmth about her that made her immediately popular, made everyone grateful to her purely for existing. She seemed to never be in a bad mood, never stressed. It was as though she felt as if life was not just easy for her, but a gift.

He'd heard that her family had moved from Sydney. That she was good at hockey and swimming, that she knew recipes for cocktails off by heart. They didn't have any classes together – she was taking drama, English, history, legal studies, easy maths – but his mates were constantly trying to get with her friends, so she was always nearby. He found himself looking for her at lunch times, in assemblies, wanting to know where she was, what she was doing, wanting to try and get closer to her. He wondered if he was so interested in her because, unlike the other girls at school, she never seemed to notice him. She never looked his way, never made eye contact with him. It wasn't until she served him at McDonald's one weekend that he realised she even knew he existed.

'I didn't know you worked here,' he'd lied as he waited for his order.

'Why would you?' she said with a laugh, as if she didn't understand why anyone would give her a second thought. He could see the blush in her cheeks. He couldn't tell if it was from him, from the heat of the chip warmers, the deep fryers, or brushed on from a compact with a name like Coral Ember or Peach Flush.

He didn't want to flatter himself but he had hope. Hope itself a privilege not all can afford.

'Well, I think it's awesome you have a job,' he said, trying to act natural, trying to sound cool.

'My parents think it's important I learn the value of money,' she said so casually he couldn't tell if she agreed with them or not.

Behind her, someone yelled, 'Big Mac!' and she turned to get it, put it in his paper bag and held the bag out to him. 'Have a great day,' she said with a smile he couldn't read. Was it sarcastic? Was it genuine? He skulked out to his car, deflated.

THAT NIGHT HE sat in his room surrounded by friends and the smoke from Scott's joint – his parents out at a charity fundraiser where the seats, he'd heard Cherie boast, were a thousand dollars apiece. He thought about Annie. Was she embarrassed he'd seen her? Embarrassed to be caught working somewhere like that? He knew she wasn't a scholarship student. They had one or two of those a year and it was always easy to tell them apart from the others. Maybe her blushing had something to do with him seeing her there? Her red cheeks gave him hope, gave him the small chub of a half-boner.

It played on his mind that that was the first and only conversation he'd had with Annie Richards. For the first time in his life, he wasn't interested in what someone thought of him, Nathan Woodward, son of Bob Woodward, but of him, Nathan

Woodward, the person. He wasn't sure why, but suddenly he needed her to know that he was not who she probably assumed he was. That he was not a snob. That even though he was one of the popular boys, he was also a person of sound moral character. From that one interaction, he knew he'd spend the rest of his life proving it to her.

He wondered, one arm draped limply around Laura McFarlane's shoulders, a bottle of beer from his parents' fridge in his hand, if this was what it felt like to be in love. He hadn't heard love explained that way. He hadn't seen it in his parents. (If anything, theirs was more a relationship of tolerance, of appearances. He had never seen his parents touch except in front of other people – and then it was hands touching on top of a table or one of Bob's hands on Cherie's lower back as he ushered her into a room. None of it natural or subtle, everything always for show.) Later that night his mouth would find Laura's and they'd kiss with too much tongue, and he'd run his hand up the inside of her thigh, put one of his fingers, then two, inside her, and think not of Laura but of Annie.

From then on, as he lay in bed at night, as he moved through the day, he thought only of Annie. About what it would be like to talk to her. To be thought of fondly by her, to be considered her equal. In the two months between deciding to win her over and kissing her behind the pool house at Adam Lancaster's party, he stopped kissing other girls, stopped pursuing them, even though James Rowlands called him a fag. His mind was set. He wanted

Annie to love him and, outside of his grades and some wins on the rugby field, this was all that mattered.

'YOU MAKE ME want to be a better person,' he told her the first time they slept together. He'd read about some things to do to her, with his hands and his mouth, ways to talk to her, and she seemed to like it.

'There are so many girls who'd kill to get with you,' she said, the bedsheet pulled up tight and tucked in snug around her armpits.

'Well, I'm not interested in them,' he said. He'd been lying on his back but he rolled over on his side to face her.

She traced the bruise on his arm from rugby practice a few days earlier.

'It looks like Florida,' she said.

'See, most of the girls at school wouldn't even know what shape Florida is.'

'You don't date someone just because they know the shape of the fourth-most populous state of America,' she said and rolled her eyes. She was smiling, though, because she knew no one else would know that either. 'And before you ask, California, Texas, New York.'

'You're not even studying geography,' he said, looking at the perfectly symmetrical shape of her face, at the way her jaw tucked down into her chin. She didn't know how beautiful she was, or, if she did, she didn't know what to do with it. That was attractive to him too.

'Yeah, but I read the news. I watch *Sale of the Century*.' She nestled into his chest and he trailed the tips of his fingers up her bare arm.

'Will you still like me if I don't get into law?' Nathan asked her. He'd been distracted lately. What if he didn't get the marks? The expectation weighed heavy.

'There is no way you're not getting in.' She ran her hand down his chest and the feel of her fingertips on his skin made him forget school, forget expectations, forget about the future he was supposed to have. 'And anyway, I'd like you no matter what job you did.' He kissed her, his hand on her face, on her shoulders, and soon he was pulling the sheet down from where she'd tucked it around her.

THAT WAS WHERE Cherie had found them: naked, in bed, giggling. Cherie, however, was not laughing. Annie had dressed quickly and Nathan accompanied her downstairs, where Cherie sat quietly at the kitchen table with her hands folded.

'Cherie, this is Annabelle Richards, from school,' he'd said awkwardly when he introduced them.

'Lovely to meet you, Mrs Woodward.' She put out a hand to shake and Cherie obliged. He was glad Annie had done that. Cherie would've respected it.

He glanced at his mother's face. Her eyes showed disapproval, but he wasn't sure if it was because he was having sex with Annie or because he was having sex with anyone at all.

Later, when they were alone at the front door, Annie's face almost blistered with embarrassment. 'Oh my god,' she said. 'Oh my GOD. That was horrible. My worst nightmare.'

'It was fine,' he tried to reassure her. 'Cherie'll be fine.' He laughed then, and Annie did too. 'Let me drive you home,' he offered, but she just shook her head.

'You need to go back in there and do damage control. I'll walk.'

'It'll be fine, I promise.' He kissed her on the head, the cheek, the neck, then the lips.

She softened, smiled. 'Talk to you later,' she said, and he watched her walk all the way down the driveway.

He stood there even once she was out of sight and watched the wind in the neighbour's palm tree, visible over the hedge. He looked at the roses, his mother's pride and joy, her only true loves. They had been trimmed down for winter, their woody stems leafless, flowerless, joyless. He was sure that, even in this state, Cherie loved those plants more than she loved him – and definitely more than she loved Fran.

When he finally found the courage to go back inside, he tried to slip past the kitchen and go straight upstairs, but Cherie called his name. He entered the kitchen slowly.

'She's in your year?'

'Yes. She wants to do commerce at Melbourne Uni,' he said. 'Major in marketing.'

'Marketing,' Cherie replied sardonically. 'I don't remember meeting her parents.'

'You haven't,' he said. 'She moved here from Sydney at the start of the year.'

Cherie nodded and Nathan could tell that as soon as she'd dismissed him she was going to get on the phone and ask questions. She'd probably have the Richards's bank statements by the end of the week.

It was only in his thirties that he'd started to wonder what had happened to make his mother behave that way. He knew it was a cliché, but maybe it was her own mother, a woman he'd never met and about whom he knew very little. She was a name on birthday cards sent from England for the first few years of his life and then she was nothing. More likely, though, it was being married to his father, who, Nathan had realised in his early teens was a terrible bore. And who, he would come to realise in time, was domineering, patronising, sexist and, despite what Bob himself thought, not actually very smart.

A FEW MONTHS after she'd walked in on Nathan and Annie, Cherie found Nathan sitting on the end of his bed crying. She stood at the door and watched him, waited for him to explain himself. They'd been mostly careful, hadn't they? But somehow, Annie was pregnant. He felt terrible, scared, stupid. How could they have been so stupid? He'd thought nothing like this could ever happen to him, that bad things didn't happen to people like him.

'I'm such an idiot,' he said, throwing himself back onto his bed dramatically.

Cherie didn't sit beside him, she didn't console him. She turned, left the room and came back a few minutes later with a cheque for a thousand dollars in a sealed envelope. It was made out to Annie. She cashed it, paid at the clinic, then the two of them split the rest. His memories of that day were foggy: three protesters outside the clinic with signs; how resolute they'd both been; the cold white waiting room and a basket of old *National Geographic* magazines. They hadn't talked about it much afterwards; they just got on with things. Like it was nothing more than a speed hump on the long road of their lives.

He thought about it too often now. What could've been. All the what-ifs piling up like a serial killer's body count.

•

NATHAN LEANED BACK on the sofa, the beer doing nothing to ease the tight knot inside him. All the love and the guilt and the grief were wound tightly together. He thought of a picture he'd seen once: a mass of mummified rats with their tails so knotted they couldn't escape, couldn't agree on a way to go to get food or a way to separate, so they all died stuck together. This was a thing that could happen in nature. When he first saw the picture he didn't believe it, but now – now he was sure there was nothing so terrible, so awful, so hard that it couldn't be true.

Seven

ANNIE STOOD NAKED IN FRONT of the mirror as water dripped from her skin, reddened by the shower.

She spent time like this often: a slow breathing in of her own body, as if every day she needed to remember she was real, that she was skin and bones, not air, not smoke.

She ran a finger along the scar. If her body was the only proof she was real, then this was the only evidence her son had existed. Sometimes she felt as if all her sadness was stored in that fold of skin, nestled in the place he used to be. A pink joker's mouth, still numb at the edges.

Eight

EV LAY ON HER SOFA for twelve minutes. She got up, drank water from the kitchen tap, then lay on the floor. She felt like she'd lived two full days: a school day and a Nathan and Annie day.

Time felt hollowed out as if with a melon baller or an ice-cream scoop. Time felt like a rolling marble. There were only twenty-four hours in a day, yet she lived thirty-six of them, forty-eight. Sometimes, at the end of the day, she would struggle to understand how she was supposed to summon the energy to get home and feed herself. How she was supposed to look after her friends, see her mother, see her brother, mark assignments and tests, plan lessons, exercise, pay bills, watch a television show, read a book, worry about climate change, go out, talk to a stranger. Things had felt so hard in this last year. There were so many things to want, so many things to fix, to learn, but right now, early on this Friday evening, energy to do only this. To lie down in the stillness of her empty flat with its cream walls, its voluptuous monstera, its huge woven wall hanging. ('It's a fibre sculpture,' Annie had said when Ev unwrapped it on her birthday a few years ago, back when these things were cool, back when this was a thing Annie thought she couldn't live without.)

Her phone buzzed, vibrating violently against the floor.

'What now?' Ev whispered. 'Please just leave me alone.'

She picked it up, looked at the screen.

'Hey, Mum,' she said into the phone.

'Just checking in,' Christine said.

In the last year, Christine had been checking in more often, more than she ever had when Ev was younger. She'd resented it at first but had learned to be grateful for it, for her mum's singsong voice that jangled like a bracelet. 'How are you?'

'I don't know,' Ev said. She wanted to say: *Sometimes I think I'm fine. Sometimes I think I'm dying. Sometimes I don't know what to do with all this pain.* She'd asked her therapist, 'How much is it possible to handle?' And her therapist had replied, with a small smile, 'Well, that depends on what you mean by handle.'

'Just remember: the things that don't kill us only make us stronger, darl,' Christine said.

Her voice sounded far away. Ev could tell she was in the car, probably driving home from work. Just the one job since she met

Greg on RSVP. They'd moved in together quickly and things were easier for Christine now; Ev was glad for it.

'I don't know if I agree with that,' Ev said. The floor was cold against her back; the rigidity of it felt good, felt like it was straightening her spine, righting some wrongs. 'It's like when you tell someone who's just been shat on by a bird that it's good luck.'

'I know, love. But sometimes we tell ourselves the things we need to believe. It's how we survive.'

Ev was quiet as she let that sink in.

'You'll be okay tomorrow. The build-up is always worse than the day itself – that's what I found after your gran. The weeks leading up to it knocked me for six, but it's just another day. Every day is just another day.'

'Thanks, Mum,' Ev said. In the last light of the room she could see a smear of dirt across her pant leg, something stuck to the bottom of her shoe. 'I'll be okay.'

'Give Annie and Nath my love,' Christine said.

'I will,' Ev replied, but she knew she wouldn't pass it on. What was the point? All the thoughts, the prayers, the well wishes weren't going to bring him back.

'Here if you need,' Christine said.

'I know. Thank you.'

'Lots of love,' Christine said before she hung up. 'Lots of love.'

Ev put the phone down on the floor beside her. She wondered if Greg kissed Christine when she arrived home, if he was happy to see her. She hoped so. She hoped he made her happy – or, if not happy, brought her comfort, one of the many things her mum had gone without for so long. She hoped that, thanks to Greg, Christine would get to retire in a few years and do all the things she hadn't been able to when she was raising two kids in that tiny unit, working three jobs just to keep the lights on. Ev imagined her reading romance novels, planting colourful flowers in pots in a wide-brimmed hat. A drive to Queensland in a caravan. Maybe Ev would have enough money to take her to Bali one day.

Ev sat up. She listened to the quiet sounds of the neighbourhood: the rattle of a tram; two women talking as they walked down the street; the heady, thumping bass of a car stereo turned right up.

Sometimes she tried to tell herself that it was impossible to feel lonely when surrounded by so much outside noise. That there were people everywhere. Loneliness was a state of mind. That she didn't need someone. That her wants were not this basic. She was a strong, independent woman. The affirmations on rotation in her mind like hits on a commercial radio station. But then she'd climb into bed and her aloneness would feel palpable; it would feel textured like an old glove.

She pulled herself up off the floor. She had forty-five minutes until she had to leave. In the shower, she ran a razor up her legs, making wide paths through the suds. She did her armpits too. Her pubes, sprouting down her thighs in two wide koala ears, were a lost cause, she decided.

Wrapped in a towel, Ev closed the bedroom blinds. The quiet of her flat made her even more aware of the pace of her heartbeat, of her nerves. She wanted to be surrounded by familiar voices, she needed distraction. She opened her laptop on her bed and, in the browser, opened the link she had saved on her bookmark bar.

She scrolled through the episodes and chose one at random. Season ten. She hadn't watched any season ten for a while. She pressed play, paused just as the screen turned black to let it load so it wouldn't buffer. She talked along with the opening lines as she picked through her wardrobe for something to wear.

'*In the criminal justice system . . .*'

Then the theme music, as familiar to her as air. In the last year, it had been one of the only things that had calmed her. She sang: 'Bum bowm na na na na naaaaa.'

She was glad her students couldn't see her, she was glad no one could see her. She knew that her aloneness offered a freedom she didn't want to live without. She thought of that Louisa May Alcott quote she'd read once, that 'liberty is a better husband than love to many of us'. She'd thought about getting it tattooed on her somewhere so that in the years to come she'd see the blurry writing, ink leached into her skin, and she'd remember she was lucky.

She picked out a pair of jeans, her most expensive t-shirt. The detectives on screen interviewed a rape victim at a hospital – her face all cut up, bruised, some of her ribs cracked. Previously it wouldn't have bothered her, the hospital scene, but now she skipped forward by ten seconds, fifteen, until they were back out on the street.

She'd only been to a hospital once before last year, when Justin, her brother, had to have his arm X-rayed after a tumble at footy practice. She'd done her maths homework on the floor of the waiting room while they put the cast on, wrapping it up in layers of white. It was eleven o'clock by the time they got home, her mum anxious that she'd missed a shift, worried about who'd look after Justin tomorrow when she was supposed to be at work.

Now, when she saw the white walls, the curtains between the beds, all she could think about was that night a year ago.

•

THE HOSPITAL STAFF had found them a small room to cry in. You rarely see anyone crying in hospitals, Ev realised. They're always tucked away in private. Crying is bad advertising for hospitals. Good advertising for airports.

Ev had a phone call to make but she couldn't bear to do it in front of anyone. She imagined them hearing her on the phone: what would they think of her? What if she didn't do it right? Al sat there on the sofa, his long legs stretching so far out in front of him that everyone had to step over them to come and go, to make tea or coffee with water from the pump-top urn.

Annie and Nathan were gone for a long time and Ev felt adrift without them, without the guidance of their horror. How sad was she allowed to be? How much pain was she allowed to feel? They – the parents – were the buoys in this ocean of grief, the lighthouses.

There were blankets draped over the arms of the sofa. One had fallen and was in a messy heap. It would stay that way until after they left. Until a nurse or a cleaner picked it up, refolded it. Ev didn't know if it would be washed or just put back in place.

Claire kept entering and leaving the room in a cloud of busy air. When she was there, she'd pace in the small space, flipping her phone over and over in her hand as if she was waiting for an important call, as if she was desperate for information because facts were all that would settle her, facts were all she had. But there was only one fact that was important and that was that he was dead.

He was dead.

He was dead.

Ev swallowed hard. She became aware of her breath, the patterns of it, the way it moved her whole torso, how it hurt if she held it for too long, how the muscles around her diaphragm contracted and expanded. How it all seemed so simple, so intuitive, until it wasn't. How someone could be alive and then be dead. How it was life's only certainty and yet it still surprised us. Still pulled the rug out from under us.

'I'm going to make some calls,' she said to Al, who looked at her as if he hadn't heard what she'd said but nodded all the same.

The hall was quiet save for the nearby bleep of a heart rate monitor. Ev walked the length of it. Up to the nurses' station and back again, around to the sofas by the lift. She sat. The pattern of the chair's fabric looked like a businessman's cheap tie. It scratched the back of her legs. She regretted the shorts she'd worn: too short for her thighs. She wished she was in jeans and a big jumper, in leggings, in pyjamas. She wished she was in bed, in the ocean, in a different country, a different life. Anywhere but here now, having to do this.

She unlocked her phone, opened her address book. The only one-to-one communication they'd ever had was a few emails about the family-friendly bridal shower Ev had organised. Her responses coming quickly and succinctly. Her disapproval of all of Ev's choices conveyed clearly through her tone. She tapped the screen, held the phone up to her ear. It rang eight times before it was answered.

'Mrs Woodward, Cherie, it's Evelyn. I'm sorry for calling so late but I'm at the hospital. There's been an accident.'

THEY DIDN'T LEAVE the hospital until after three. A taxi took them back to Nathan and Annie's to get it ready, to clean it up, to make it feel somehow less like the site of a tragedy, less like a war zone, less like ground zero. Though it would never not be a place where something had happened. It would never just be a kitchen again.

Ev took the key from the lockbox, the code the previous day's date, his birthday, the day he died. She let them in. The lights were still on. The back door wide open. Moths and little flies were flocking around the downlights in the living room.

Ev cleaned up the glasses outside, shoved the butt of the joint into a half-empty can of beer. Then she turned off the outside lights, closed the bi-fold door.

In the kitchen, Al and Claire were standing silently, staring at the floor as if frozen in time, unable to move. At their feet was the scattered detritus the paramedics had left behind. Claire took the bag out of the kitchen bin and held it open while Al sank to his knees and gathered up strange bits of plastic and the wrappers of things, discarded tape.

Ev surveyed the rest of the mess. Half-eaten sausage rolls and empty bottles, the rest of the birthday cake uncovered, drying out. She took a roll of tin foil from the kitchen drawer and covered it, squeezed it into the fridge beside bowls of soggy lettuce from the last of the salads, a platter of fruit. Over by the table were the leftover lolly bags, the contents of one of them littered across the floor. Worms, dinosaurs, marshmallows sprayed like bullet casings. Evidence of her crime. She needed them gone. Ev got down on her knees and began sweeping the lollies into her hands frantically. She worried that if she didn't get rid of them as quickly as possible, she was going to be sick. She swept and swept but somehow they were getting wet, somehow they were so sticky. It wasn't until Al and Claire picked her up off the floor, held her between them, that she realised she was crying. They stood there in the kitchen in that hug for a long time. Ev could've stayed there for a week, for a whole year, but instead they broke away, somehow revived. They finished the cleaning.

She declined the offer to sleep on Al and Claire's sofa bed, instead sharing an Uber home with them, Claire insisting they drop her off first.

'There's nothing more depressing than being alone in an Uber when you're sad,' Claire said.

'I think crying alone in an Uber affects your rating too,' Al said.

Ev managed a smile.

Claire held her hand the whole way up Nicholson Street.

'What do we do next?' Ev asked. 'What do we do tomorrow?'

'I don't know,' Claire said. 'We go over there, I guess.'

Al was silent in the front seat. Ev nodded.

The car slowed to a stop. She turned to Claire and they hugged again, a damp hug, faces, shoulders, hair glittering with tears. When she slid out of the back of the car, Al was standing waiting. He wrapped his long arms around her. He smelled of sweat, of coffee and hospitals, the buttery depths of sadness.

'Will you be okay?' Al asked.

'No,' she said, laughing between her tears. 'But I guess so.'

'Call us if you need anything. If you change your mind and want to come over. Anything. We'll leave our phones on.'

'I will,' Ev said.

He slid into the back of the car. As they drove away, she saw him put his arm around Claire.

SHE DRIFTED THROUGH the dark flat, guided by a streetlight, by muscle memory. In the bathroom, she pulled the string for the light and looked in the mirror. She was almost surprised to see that her hair hadn't greyed from the shock, that her eyes were still brown. She looked exhausted. As if she'd been broken and stuck back together with glue.

She brushed her teeth, washed her face, applied the expensive face oil to her cheeks. Her skin felt like it belonged to someone else. She opened her eyes and hoped to see someone else's face, hoped to wake up from this terrible nightmare in someone else's life. She wanted it not to be true, not to be real.

She froze at the door to the kitchen when she saw the dust on the kitchen table, illuminated by the glow of the streetlight. She'd put the empty lolly packets in the bin before she left, but she'd run out of time to wipe the surface and so there it sat: the icing sugar dust from inside the packets. Residue of the marshmallows she'd put in the lolly bags to pad them out; the fine-grained evidence of fault.

She crumpled to the floor. She couldn't breathe. She sat there, pressed up against the wooden leg of the table, next to the metal leg of the chair, until daylight came. Until she was able to pick herself up, shower, and go back to Annie and Nathan's.

Days, weeks later, she could still feel the indentations of the wood and the metal in her skin.

A year later, she still wore that day in her body as if she'd absorbed it. The guilt, the agonising pain: she carried it under her skin like a bruise. Tender, purpling.

•

MOISTURISING HER LEGS, Ev found a spiky spot on each knee, one on her ankle and a whole stripe up her calf that she'd missed. She didn't have time to fix it. It didn't matter anyway.

As she applied deodorant to her underarms, Stabler and Benson chatted to a suspect. A man, always a man. He was traditionally good-looking in that American, boof-haired, button-up shirt way. She'd met dozens of lawyers like him. CEOs, CFOs. Sometimes, in meetings, she used to work out how many nurses' salaries could be paid with the profits of each deal she helped negotiate. How many teachers'. How much affordable housing could be built, how many trees could be planted. The amount of injustice in the world made her sick.

Maybe that's why she liked these shows? In the end justice often prevailed. Within forty minutes everything was tied in a neat bow. More often than not, the bad guy paid, the credits rolled and everything was right with the world.

Ev smoothed foundation onto her cheeks with her fingers, then wiped her hand on the towel that sat in a wet heap on her bed. She'd almost definitely forget to hang it up before she left and end up with a damp bed when she inevitably came home after two drinks, disappointed. Was it wrong that she wanted justice in real life too? That she wanted everything to be right with the world, to be tied in a neat bow?

She opened her mouth and drew a reddish-orange lipstick across her lips. She smacked them together and let herself believe it was possible. That maybe, for once, it could be possible.

Nine

ON THE TRAIN AL REMEMBERED you're supposed to bring a gift to a housewarming. If Claire were there, she'd have organised something, somehow fitting not just the thought of buying something into her busy day but the action of it too. That had always amazed him about her: the amount of room in her head for all the things she had to think about.

Al rocked back and forth with the motion of the train, trying to stay upright, trying not to be sick. Between leaving the office and finding himself back on a train, he'd watched a movie. A ten thirty session of that Lady Gaga film he'd refused to go see with Claire. He cried through the whole second half, alone in the dark. Afterwards, blinking in the sunlight of the hot afternoon, he'd found somewhere open, ordered a bloody mary, and drank it sitting alone at the bar. He'd turned his phone off before the movie and was too scared to turn it back on. Too scared of what Katrina would say about him walking out. He'd done the bare minimum of his job over the last year, missing most of his deadlines, only just making budget. There had to come a point where barely enough was no longer good enough. Perhaps this was it. Perhaps today. The second of November. The second, the second, the second. He cursed it under his breath as though the date were at fault for today, for tomorrow, for the six pints he'd had after the bloody mary. As though the date were at fault for his growing irritation at the time the train was taking, for the noise the train was making.

'Don't,' Al said to Zahra as she opened the door to her brother's apartment. 'I know I'm late.'

She held her hands up in mock surrender. 'You smell like a brewery,' she said, taking the pot plant out of his hands. It left a muddy streak across the front of his t-shirt. He hadn't noticed that the pot was filthy when he'd swiped it from the front porch of one of the houses between the station and Javeed's apartment block.

He left his shoes in the pile by the door, then Zahra dragged him down the hall and pushed him towards the first doorway, which led to the bathroom.

'Go and freshen up before anyone else gets a whiff of you,' she said. Down the hall, he heard her yell, 'Ali brought you a plant!' Everyone cheered. At least Javeed's apartment was on the fifth floor, which meant there was no chance the neighbours Al stole it from would spot it on his cousin's balcony.

He looked around the bathroom. It resembled every bathroom in every new-build apartment block in Australia. A cold colour scheme of charcoal and white, stainless-steel fixtures. Boxy. Quickly and shoddily constructed.

It was an apartment bought off the plan. Al knew this because Javeed had texted him, called him, emailed him, Facebook messaged him throughout every stage of the looking, borrowing and buying process, despite the fact that Al had never owned a house. Al guessed this was how brothers acted, what they did for each other. Weren't they practically brothers, after all?

Javeed was the baby of the family, three years his and Zahra's junior. He was annoying. A gnocchi chin and that slicked-back hair, his little ponytail, his shaved undercut. He'd been annoying since birth. A bad sleeper, a fussy toddler. Al's clearest memories from childhood involved getting frustrated with Javeed's indecision. From which flavour Paddle Pop he wanted (he'd once spent twenty-five minutes in the corner store deliberating between banana, chocolate and rainbow, until the owner of the store kicked them out and no one got an ice cream), to which character he wanted to be in Mario Kart on N64 (it didn't matter; Al beat him every single time). Javeed had been plagued by indecision his whole life. When he'd called to say he'd finally settled on an apartment, Al couldn't believe it. Standing in it now, the reality of it depressed him. All that back and forth, all that money, for this little box, for these grey tiles, for this shallow bath. The system was broken.

Al looked at himself in the bathroom mirror. There was dirt down the front of his t-shirt, a streak of it too big for his jacket to hide. A smear of it across his cheek too. His eyes were bloodshot, still ringed by the dark circles that'd arrived a year ago and settled in. He looked a mess.

He stood over the sink and tried to wipe the dirt off. He splashed water on his face, washed his hands, dried them on a hand towel that was already wet from the hands of others. He pushed on the corner of the mirror and it popped open. He examined the pill bottles inside: Finasteride (he made a mental note to google that later), vitamins for healthy hair growth and prostate health, Xanax. He picked up some Listerine, swished it around in his mouth, gargled, spat. He needed to pull himself together. To hold himself together just long enough to have dinner and get home.

He opened the Xanax, popped a pill in his pocket for later, put it back in the cupboard, straightened his shoulders and stepped out into the hall.

The next room along was the bedroom. Al looked at it from the doorway. It was tiny, almost all bed, with a mirrored built-in. Al was surprised by Javeed's choice of bed linen – a tropical, floral pattern with birds of paradise, palm fronds. On the wall, a painting of a green sea turtle; on the bedside table, a framed photo of the three of them as kids: Al and Zahra and Javeed. They looked like siblings, with the same wide faces, same big brown eyes. He headed for the open-plan living area, curious to see more of his younger cousin's decorating flair.

'Ali!' Leila grabbed him by the lapels and kissed him on each cheek before he'd even made it into the room. 'What time do you call this?'

'Sorry, Aunty,' he said. She looked thin, the patterned scarf on her head not for modesty but for dignity. He didn't realise the chemo had made her lose her hair. He wanted to know if it had fallen out in clumps or if Zahra had helped her shave it. He wanted to know how she was, how she felt in her body, in her mind, in her faith. Was she scared? Al knew he was too scared to ask; the words stayed in his throat as if blocked by a plug.

'Oh, I know, it's ghastly,' Leila said, catching him staring. She put her hand to her head self-consciously.

'You look beautiful,' he said. 'As always.' He put his arm around her shoulders.

'Oh stop it,' she said, but she let him hold her for a few seconds before pushing him off playfully.

Javeed was standing in the kitchen: dark grey cupboards, a big silver fridge.

'Congratulations, cousin.' Al kissed Javeed's cheeks, slapped his back as they pressed their torsos together in an awkward hug. 'You finally did it.'

'And I did it all by myself,' Javeed said.

Al breathed deeply to calm himself. You ungrateful little shit, he thought. He recalled one particularly bad weekend when Javeed sent him sixteen texts, each with a link to a different apartment he wanted Al's thoughts on. They all looked the same to Al, but he wrote back listing pros and cons of each one.

His grandmother stopped fussing in the kitchen to greet him.

'You're late.' Bibi punched him on the arm before he bent down to kiss her, once on each cheek and a third to make up for his tardiness. She was shrinking; her body squat and round, her white hair thinning on top.

He didn't bother to make an excuse. He let her tap him on the cheek, her soft palm against his beard. He'd always been her favourite. She'd forgive him.

Al moved to his uncle next, kissed both Navid's cheeks. It would just be the six of them tonight. His father wasn't there, of course. Al felt relieved when he didn't show up, then guilty for feeling relieved.

Al stood quietly next to Navid, the two of them watching as Zahra and Leila pulled tin foil off platters of food, counted out plates and cutlery. Al looked at his uncle, the man who'd practically raised him. He looked smaller, tense. Was it the toll of Leila's cancer coming back, the treatment, the waiting that was making his shoulders stoop?

Leila and her sister had married tall men. His dad just shy of six foot three, Navid six two. Zahra was five ten, Al the tallest. It was only Javeed who missed out somehow. He was so short when he was younger that his parents had taken him to get X-rays of his wrist bones, they were so worried he'd never grow. It happened eventually. He woke up one morning and was five foot seven, the same height as Kurt Cobain, or so he liked to remind them. That didn't stop Al from making fun of him, calling him 'short stuff', 'short stop' until Javeed ran to Leila, who'd give Al a stern talking-to. 'Your mother would be very disappointed in your behaviour,' she would tell him, or, 'What would your mother say about this?' The truth was Al didn't know what his mother would've thought about anything. He was so young when she died that he could barely remember her. Sometimes he'd hear her feathery voice in his dreams, or see the colours she wore: deep magentas, crimsons, pinks. But she was more like a collage of a person than a real person to him, an image made up of photos, memories, the stories others told, all stuck together to form a whole. His dad was like a ghost now, too. His skin prickled, his ears hummed when he thought of it.

'Where's that lovely girlfriend of yours?' Leila called to him from across the room.

'Mama, I told you – she's working late,' Zahra said.

Al couldn't remember mentioning the dinner to Claire. He tried to remember the last family dinner she'd come to. She used to love them; her and Zahra giggling like co-conspirators down one end of the table, Javeed trying his best to flirt. Even Bibi softened around Claire, hinting at her desire for a wedding and babies. Claire used to fob it off with a laugh but they'd always talk about it in bed after. Talk about when and how, what the plan was. They hadn't had that conversation in a while.

'Oh, yes! Sorry: chemo brain.' Leila tapped herself on the head, rolled her eyes.

Al steadied himself against the kitchen bench and looked around properly.

The room was decorated in what Claire would've described as 'bachelor style'. There was a squat black leather sofa with silver legs, a hard back and sides. It looked like it was more for show than for comfort. You couldn't lie on it, Al thought. Or at least he couldn't; Javeed would probably fit. Be nice to your cousin, he chided himself. Just get through it.

He was sure every apartment in this building was a version of the same thing; he figured you'd pay extra for another box of a bedroom, a bit more light, for a view of either a busy street or the backyards of people who thought they were buying into the privacy that suburbia once guaranteed, but otherwise each of them would look exactly the same.

'Come on, let's eat, this is going cold,' Zahra said. The glass dining table was covered with food: chicken and lamb stews, a tahdig. They had Bibi and Leila written all over them.

Leila accompanied Bibi to the table, poured her a drink. Al took a seat, a small metal stool dragged in from the balcony to accommodate all of them. Al doubted there'd ever be this many people in the apartment again. Maybe some of Javeed's annoying mates would come over to watch sport on the enormous TV. He wondered if Javeed would bring girls back here. The thought of it made him queasy.

Leila poured everyone a glass of Coke.

'Nooshe-jaan,' Javeed said, and reached for the stew nearest him.

Al guzzled his drink in a few sips, poured himself another.

'This looks beautiful, Mama,' Zahra said, spooning rice onto a plate and passing it to Leila, who made a plate for Bibi before she served herself.

'How do you know I didn't cook it all?' Javeed said defensively.

'Your oven still has the plastic lining on it,' Al said without missing a beat.

Javeed laughed so loudly it sounded forced. 'So can you believe it, Ali?' he asked. 'This is all mine!' He gestured around at the white walls.

'Mostly the bank's,' Al said.

'You and Claire could get yourselves one of these,' Navid suggested.

'That'd be nice,' Leila said encouragingly.

Al imagined living in the same boxy apartment. Feeling this same claustrophobia.

'You should!' Javeed said enthusiastically. 'We could hang out all the time. The one next door is still empty.'

'We're saving up for a house,' Al said.

'Nah, come on! There are bigger apartments upstairs, two bedrooms.'

'We need something with a garden for Crunchie.'

'Forget the cat,' Javeed said. Zahra, Bibi and Leila glared at him. 'You don't even like cats.'

'I like this cat,' Al said quietly, sternly, his irritation spiking.

'Just let it go out in the neighbourhood when you move in here. Someone will take it in.' Javeed's voice was getting louder, as it always did when he thought he was being funny, when he thought he was the life of the party.

'I don't want to live in this apartment block,' Al said sharply.

'Come on, you two,' Navid said in his gentle voice.

'Put some biscuits on the road, wait for a car to come along.' Javeed dusted off his hands as if to say, *Job done, cat taken care of.*

The thought of losing Crunchie, after everything else. Al felt his blood roll to a boil. His fists tingled. 'You're a psycho,' he snapped.

'Well at least I'm not a drunk,' Javeed said, sitting back in his chair.

Al looked at his cousin's smug face, and before he even knew what he was doing, he was out of his seat, moving across the room, he was lunging at Javeed, he was being dragged off him, a scuffle of bodies around him, two pairs of hands. He felt his fist swipe at his cousin, who had pushed his chair back just in time and stood, cowering, out of Al's reach.

'Get him off me,' Javeed screamed, even though Zahra and Navid were already holding Al.

Zahra pushed Al by the chest, then, when he turned, she pushed him all the way out onto the balcony, her hands on his back. As he passed Bibi and Leila, they averted their eyes, but he could see both of them were upset.

Al leaned forward, folded his arms on the balcony's railing and looked out over the suburbs, little lights, little lives twinkling. He was aware of Zahra standing silently behind him. He took four deep breaths. He looked down at his hands. Neither of them hurt, no bloody knuckles. Nothing broken. He'd swung and missed. He was grateful for that. He was terrified of turning around, terrified of going back inside. So much for keeping himself together. He was in pieces.

'Well?' he heard Zahra say.

He turned around, avoiding her gaze. Inside, Leila and Bibi were fussing over Javeed, Navid was shaking his head. Amid it all, Javeed looked over at Al and smiled.

'What the fuck was that?' Zahra spat out in a whisper, but didn't wait for an answer. 'We don't do that, Al. Not in this family.'

'I know,' he said, he dropped his head into his hands. 'I'm sorry.'

'Don't say sorry to me,' she said, and then stopped, corrected herself. 'No, wait – do. Say sorry to me, to Mum and Dad, to Bibi and to Javeed. Then you have to deal with this before it eats you up inside or gets you killed.'

'It won't,' Al said. 'It's not going to get that bad.'

'You just tried to punch my little brother. I think it's already that bad.'

'He was deliberately antagonising me,' Al said, trying to shift the blame. 'Crunchie.' He teared up. Javeed was right, he'd never really liked cats that much, but Crunchie wasn't just any cat. He loved her. He couldn't lose another thing. He couldn't.

'He's a dickhead, sure,' Zahra said. 'But I will not put up with violence of any kind. If you don't go and get help, then you will not be welcome in my home or my family's homes again.' She was yelling at him now, and he could do nothing but hang his head and take it. He knew her well enough to know this was not an empty threat. 'And where did you get that ugly plant?' she asked – a joke, he thought, to show that she was done berating him, to show she cared.

'Number twenty-one,' Al said, and laughed a little out of embarrassment for the plant, for his behaviour, for himself. He wondered if it were possible for him to climb down the balcony, if there was a drainpipe that would take his weight. Maybe he could jump and only break an ankle. Anything to avoid the glare of his grandmother, the disappointment of his aunt, the glee on the face of his cousin.

'Al,' she said despairingly. 'We're going to go inside and you're going to apologise to everyone. You're going to eat your dinner, you're going to take that plant back, you're going to stop drinking so much, you're going to talk to someone.' She paused, softened her tone slightly. 'I know you've had all these bad things happen one after another and I know anniversaries are tough. I know. It's not fair. But you have to get your shit together.'

She was standing close to him now, a hand on his shoulder. Their mothers had children within months of each other; now the same cancer was coming for Leila thirty years later. He'd been acting like he was the only one who'd been the victim of rotten luck. Shame hit him quickly, sat on his skin uneasy like water.

'Take a deep breath, pull yourself together, then come back inside. You're a good man, and I love you, but this ends now.' She walked back inside without him.

Through the window, Al could see Leila staring at him. Bibi sat eating small spoonfuls of rice. She appeared to be praying between mouthfuls. She wouldn't let him live this down in a hurry. This would be a stain on their family for a long time. You fucking idiot, he thought. Zahra was right.

He took two steps inside and the room fell silent.

'Please don't hit me,' Javeed said in mock fear and Al breathed in and out, just to stop the rage from simmering up and over again.

'Al, apologise to your cousin.' Zahra stood with her hands on her hips.

Al started to speak but stopped. All eyes were on him, Javeed's glinting as if this was the best day of his life. Al hesitated.

'Do it,' she commanded.

'I'm sorry,' Al said. 'I haven't been myself lately, but there was no excuse for that. It'll never happen again.'

Zahra nodded at him, assuaging very little of the guilt and shame that grumbled inside him like hunger. 'Now it's your turn, Javeed,' she said. 'Apologise to your cousin.'

'Me?' Javeed whined. 'But I didn't do anything. He attacked me. He assaulted me; I should call the poli—'

'Javeed.' Bibi cut him off, and that's when Al knew it was serious, that he was really in trouble – they both were. Bibi was shaking her head, muttering quietly.

'Sorry, Al,' Javeed said. 'You are not a drunk.'

Al mouthed 'thank you' to his cousin, even though he knew there was some truth to his accusation.

'Can we sit down and enjoy this meal as a family now, please? It's all I want,' Leila said, her bottom lip wobbling a little as it did in every movie she ever watched, during every episode of *Home and Away*.

'I'm sorry, Leila; I'm sorry, Bibi,' Al said, and his grandmother looked up from her plate for just a few seconds. Just long enough for him to know he was not forgiven, not yet. He knew he'd have to do something big to win back her affection. Propose to Claire, perhaps.

They took their seats at the table and started eating silently. Al's plate was still empty. He realised he hadn't eaten all day – unless you counted the celery stick in his bloody mary as food. He felt like he was sobering up. He felt regretful, ravished by hunger. He spooned some of the lamb stew onto his plate, the garlicky yoghurt sauce, a chunk of the crispy top of the tahdig, the best bit.

He was pretty sure Javeed would never let him live this down (he imagined future family gatherings: 'Remember that time you tried to hit me?'), but he did know that he'd never let it happen again. That he'd try to do better. He'd drink less. Maybe he'd get up early with Claire in the mornings and meditate. Maybe maybe maybe.

He wondered if Zahra would tell Claire. He hoped not. He hoped she'd never find out. He was scared of how Claire would react, scared she'd leave, that she'd become another name on the long list of people he'd lost, another thing he'd regret for the rest of his life.

Ten

ANNIE CAME DOWNSTAIRS, HER WET hair twisted up in a towel, her pyjamas already on. Nathan turned to see her paused at the door, staring out into the back garden, to the sky beyond him. She felt so far away from him. Sometimes he'd watch her out the back. From the kitchen, from upstairs. She'd stand for whole minutes at a time. So pale and still she looked like a statue carved out of marble.

'Hey,' he said and watched her attention shift slowly to him. She did everything so much more slowly these days.

'Hey,' Annie said and came to sit beside him on the sofa. She didn't look at him, but he looked at her. Like him, she'd lost weight. She'd always been thin; never had to worry about what she ate. But her face looked different now – paler, cheekbones sharper, as if the grief had changed the shape of her.

'I –' she started, then stopped, made the noise of air leaving a balloon.

'You don't have to –' Nathan said.

The silence was excruciating.

'Have you seen the Cunninghams' garden, the one on the corner?'

He nodded.

'I had a moment of madness, I guess. Where' – her voice trembled – 'where I thought that maybe if I –'

'You don't have to.' Nathan wasn't sure he could bear to hear it.

'I need to say it,' Annie said. 'Let me say it.' She took a deep breath, kept going. 'I thought that maybe if our garden looked more like theirs, then maybe he wouldn't have died; maybe we'd have a garden full of mess and toys and life, and he'd be here playing in it. And I know . . .' She groaned and sat forward, her face in her hands. 'You don't have to say anything. I know it sounds wild.'

'I'm sure it made sense at the time,' he said and reached out to pat her knee. He felt her stiffen at his touch and it made his skin go cold. 'We'll get someone in to fix it. It's okay.'

Nathan drained the last of his beer, fought the temptation to take another from the fridge.

'We're supposed to be having dinner in Toorak tonight,' he said, taking the glass necks of his beer and Ev's between the fingers of one hand. He stood, took them to the bin.

'Oh god, I forgot.'

'Me too – she called to remind me. You don't have to come.'

'I don't know if I can face it tonight,' Annie said. 'Would you mind?'

'It's okay,' he said, walking towards her. She'd unwound the towel from her wet hair and was drying the ends. He kissed the top of her head. 'It's okay,' he said, and he picked his keys up from the kitchen bench and walked out past the mess of a garden and through the gate.

IT WAS STILL light. It would be light until late. Before, they would've put him to bed and sat out on the deck and had a glass of wine together while the sky turned pink then darkened to black. Before, there was a nightly ritual, a schedule, a sun around which their world turned. Nathan hadn't known how much he should've relished those times; he hadn't known how short-lived they'd be, how few of them they'd get. He knew the way the Joni Mitchell song went, the old adage that turned out to be true.

The error they'd made, Nathan realised (one of many), was that they let themselves make plans for the future. They let themselves imagine what life could be like a week, two weeks, six months, five years down the track. They'd imagined a future for their family, three of them first, then maybe four one day?

He hadn't known then what he knew now: that the future didn't exist.

You could make all the plans in the world, but nothing was certain.

He pulled up at the end of the long driveway. The house was hidden from the street by a tall green hedge. Behind it, a perfectly manicured lawn. Roses. That house. Painted white, two storeys, always cold.

Ev referred to it as the Palace, Bob and Cherie as the King and Queen, or Sir and Lady, the Duke and Duchess of Toorak.

He had to fight the urge to drive away. To turn around in the cul-de-sac at the end of the street and go home, go anywhere else. He turned in, parked behind Cherie's gold Mercedes and sat in the car while the engine cooled. He pulled out his phone and watched the cards fall into place on the green background. He liked how reliable they were. Fifty-two of them every time. No surprises, no curve balls. A five on a six. An ace up top. A black king. It unfolded quickly, easily, a distraction of numbers, suits and colours. And then he was stuck. Three kings out, the fourth behind a six he couldn't budge.

'Fuck it,' he said and closed the app. He looked up at the house as a wave of dread washed over him. 'Come on,' he said to himself. He was a man, a real human man, and he was going to get out of the car and go inside and get over and done with whatever he was going to have to get over and done with. He had already survived the worst thing it was possible to survive, this would be a piece of cake.

He let himself in; the door was always unlocked despite the security cameras, the clamorous alarm that hee-hawed in the night, often set off by nothing in particular.

A long, tiled hall and, at the end of it, towards the back of the house, immaculate shelves of books, ornaments he'd never been allowed to touch, sitting rooms reserved for adults, a kitchen remodelled every few years to keep up with Cherie's changing taste. This one, inspired by a trip to Italy the previous year, covered in terrazzo, marble, rose gold taps, copper pans dangling from hooks above the island.

He found Cherie sitting there alone now, on a stool, back straight, magazine open in front of her. Behind her, the oven beaming; beside her, a glass of wine and a bottle half full. This was a new thing. In the past, Cherie would rarely have more than one glass. Now she'd polish off a bottle on her own. Nathan wondered what Martha must think of this family as she sorted the recycling. Martha, one of the people they paid to keep the house looking nice, the garden looking nice.

When Nathan walked in, Cherie didn't adjust her posture, didn't stand to greet him. Even in the kitchen she had the air of a woman sitting alone in an empty ballroom. There was so much space around her, so much distance between them.

'Hello,' Nathan said, placing the bottle of chardonnay he'd bought on the way over down on the end of the long island.

'Is that all I get?' she asked, and watched as he circled the bench to stand beside her.

She offered her cheek. He kissed it; his mother's skin felt cold, powdery.

'Just you?'

'Annie wasn't feeling well,' he said, and she made a tut of disapproval. 'Dad?' he asked.

'Not here.' Cherie licked a finger to turn a page of her magazine.

Nathan felt like he was swimming in oil. He didn't have it in him to survive a dinner alone with Cherie. At least if his father were there, he'd dominate the conversation with stories about people Nathan didn't know or, if he knew them, didn't care about. Or he'd talk about things in the news about which he knew only the facts that supported his worldview. But at least there'd be noise. At least there'd be something to fill the silence other than his grief, his dread, their small talk.

'At work?' Nathan asked.

'Where else?' Cherie turned another page.

'Do you think he'll ever retire?' Nathan had never seen his mother do a day's work in her life. Working was all Bob Woodward did, all he was. He couldn't picture the two of them actually spending time together.

'You'd have to ask him that,' she said.

'Did you end up repainting the sitting room?' He was trawling the depths of his brain for questions to ask, anything that might capture her attention.

'Terracotta,' she said, and Nathan took it as an excuse to leave the room. First, he took a beer from the fridge, opened it, threw the bottle top onto the bench. He'd grown up leaving messes lying around, knowing they'd be tidied up, knowing that there were no consequences. He was the golden child. The youngest but, while his parents would never say it aloud, their only hope. Fran, four years his senior, was the scruffy tomboy, the leftie tree-hugger, now essentially an outcast.

Nathan wished she was there now. When they were kids, she acted as a buffer for him for as long as she could handle it, carried as much weight as she could bear. She was the only source of warmth in this family and was offered nothing but coldness in return.

He headed down the hall.

The sitting room – now painted in terracotta – looked over the outdoor dining areas and the lawn to the tennis court. He stood at the French doors that, in summer, were always open, and remembered the parties they'd have out there when he was a kid. A marquee erected in the garden, caterers in white shirts. He and Fran forced to dress up, forced to sit up straight and say nothing down one end of a dinner table, while at the other Bob regaled his guests with stories about business wins and close personal friends who were rich or famous or both. As they brushed their teeth at night, Fran would do impressions of his big booming voice.

He turned and walked along the shelves of books he was sure had never been opened, their spines never cracked. The ghostwritten memoirs of sports stars and politicians; a book of Monet's waterlilies purchased in Giverny, a trip Cherie and Bob took during Fran's final few months of school. Just the two of them in the house while she studied, while she took exams. She was thankful for the quiet. In between the books, photos of Cherie and Bob with dignitaries and celebrities: a now-disgraced businessman; a former PM; a cricket captain whose glory years were far behind him. It struck Nathan as pathetic: all that grandstanding.

'It warms the room up, don't you think?' Cherie asked from the door.

'You know what else might warm the room up?' Nathan said sarcastically. 'Some photos of your family. Of your grandkids, perhaps.'

'Don't do that,' Cherie said, sweeping her hand through the air as if she was brushing away a fly.

'Do what?' Nathan asked. He felt something building inside him.

'Not everything is about you,' she said.

'Oh, for fuck's sake,' Nathan spat.

He watched his mother's body stiffen, a lake freezing in time lapse.

'Show some respect,' she ordered.

'What is it about you, exactly, that I'm supposed to respect?' He willed himself to stop, but it was as if something had blown, as if he were Chernobyl and it was too late for safety switches, too late for cooling water. 'You know it's his birthday tomorrow, right? It's the anniversary of . . .' His death. He couldn't say the words. His death. His death. Death.

'Don't, Nathan.'

'Don't what? Talk about my dead son?' His face felt hot and wet, tears streaming.

'Don't bring all that into this. No one's got any more time for your feelings.'

He took a step closer to her. He had too much spit in his mouth.

'Go fuck yourself,' he said quietly. Then he stormed past her. Back up the hall. He didn't stop to close the front door, left it open, gaping.

'Where do you think you're going?' she called as she trotted after him, her heels click-clacking on the marble tiles. 'Don't you –' he heard her say, but he was gone.

He was sitting in the driver's seat by the time she caught up to him. He tried to close the door but she grabbed it, pulled it open.

'It wasn't just you,' she said coolly, calmly. She had run after him but she wasn't out of breath. 'We lost him too. Our only grandchild and we lost him too.'

He pushed her hand away and pulled the door closed, turned the key in the ignition, reversed to his right and then drove forward out into the street. He left her standing there alone.

He turned left, then right, and two streets away from his child-hood home pulled over at the side of the road. He put the park brake on and screamed and screamed and screamed until there was nothing left to come out.

Eleven

EV CHAINED HER BIKE TO a clearway sign outside the bar. She was proud she'd rallied herself and made it out on a Friday night.

She'd checked Hinge three times before she left to make sure she had the right day, the right time, the right place. She was hoping to get there first to find a good spot – where no one was close enough to hear them talk – and check her nose for boogers, her eyelids for flecks of mascara from her too-long lashes, her teeth for a smear of lipstick, but she'd spent too long getting ready. While she wasn't late, she felt hurried, out of breath, her clothes skew-whiff.

She looked down at her phone. A message from a number she didn't have saved had arrived while she'd been riding.

I'm early. I'll be the dork reading at the bar.

Her fingers tingled with nerves. She straightened her clothes and, from the street, peered through the window into the dimly lit bar. Emily sat on a stool in an Alpha60 dress, shaped like a silk cocoon. Her sandalled feet rested on the footrest, and she was looking down at her book. Beside her was a glass of wine, half drunk.

Ev hadn't told anyone she was going on a date. Normally she'd mention it to Claire and Annie in their group chat, especially if she was meeting a man. She'd take a screen grab of his profile, give a time and a location, send a text when she got home safe. But she hadn't been on many dates lately, and tonight's felt like especially poor timing. She'd agreed to it a week earlier, the only free night Emily had in her schedule. It was only when Ev went to put it in her calendar that she realised the date. Already, that date. 'What kind of person goes on a first date the night before the anniversary of their godson's death?' Ev had imagined asking her therapist. She imagined her answer: 'A healthy person.' 'A person who's doing very well under the circumstances.' 'Someone who's opening themselves up to the possibility of love.' These imaginary conversations were a vast improvement on the ones she used to have with herself, her negative self-talk replaced by the tempered, calm voice of her therapist. Ev hoped Jess was proud of her, wondered if it was problematic to want your therapist to be proud of you (wondered if this was a thing she should ask her therapist).

'Hello,' Ev said awkwardly, leaning against the bar next to Emily.

'Evelyn? Hi.' Emily slipped off the stool, smiling, and hugged her. Ev noticed her lips were heart-shaped, slicked pink.

Emily sat, dog-eared the corner of her page and closed the book. Ev looked at its cover: black and white, a large tree through the middle.

'Don't look at that,' Emily said and quickly turned the book over. 'I'm going through a weird crime phase.' She giggled, sounding nervous, embarrassed.

'No judgement here,' Ev said. 'People should be allowed to do the things that make them happy.'

'So you're not an English teacher?' Emily asked.

Ev had taken VCE English, had come top of her class, but she didn't like that things were so open to interpretation, that there were too many possible meanings. History felt final – the version of it we chose to believe, at least.

'History.'

The bartender leaned towards her.

'I'll just have whatever she's having.' Ev pointed at Emily's wineglass.

'Pinot noir,' Emily confirmed.

'So, how was your day?' Ev asked, watching Emily's lips as she described in detail the process of acquiring a new work for the gallery. She had a gap between her two front teeth. She had a lightness to her, an ease to the way she talked. She was thirty-four, her hair cut in a short dark bob, and the smooth lines of her hair, her dress, her arms, made her look so together. Emily was so pretty, Ev didn't understand why she was single, why she was here, at this blue-tiled bar on Lygon Street. Ev felt lucky. This time, she really did feel lucky.

'So do you have any exciting plans for the weekend?' Emily asked before taking a big gulp of her wine.

Ev took a deep breath; she noticed that Emily's hand was shaking, just a little.

'Well,' she started, and then paused. 'Do you want the real answer or a fake one that will make me seem more attractive?' There was no use in hiding, pretending.

'Real, one hundred per cent,' Emily said, her eyebrow raised, intrigued.

'Tomorrow is the one-year anniversary of the death of my friends' son.' Ev hadn't said it out loud for a while, and her voice wobbled a little. 'He was my godson, and I was there when it happened.'

'Oh, fuck,' Emily said. She covered her mouth with one hand. 'I'm so sorry.' She reached out instinctively, touched Ev's arm with the other.

'Yeah, thanks,' Ev said. 'He was two.' Emily was quiet for a few seconds. Ev's stomach dropped. She'd blown it.

'My brother died when I was eleven, so I kind of get it.' Emily looked down at her hands. 'I mean, it's not the same. Different bad . . . you know.' She smiled and Ev nodded. She knew.

'I'm sorry about your brother. How old was he? If you don't mind . . .'

'Not at all,' Emily said. 'He was eight. It was leukemia. So it was years of doctors' appointments and hospital visits. That poor kid – his bald little head.' Emily bit her lip.

'Oh god. That's awful.' Ev wished she'd lied about her weekend plans. She regretted bringing it up. Regretted everything.

'It's okay,' Emily said. 'It was a long time ago. So, you'll do something with your friends tomorrow?'

'We haven't made a plan, but I think I'll go over and hang out.' Ev took a sip of wine.

'You're a good friend.'

'Not really.' She shrugged. What she did felt like the bare minimum.

'No, you are,' Emily said firmly. 'I know they were only eleven, but my friends were shit when my brother died. I think their parents told them not to mention it because they were worried about upsetting me. So whenever I brought him up they just shut me down and talked about other things.'

'You poor thing,' Ev said. 'How did your parents handle –' She stopped as Annie and Nathan flashed before her eyes. 'Sorry, that's a stupid question.'

'It's not.' Emily smiled kindly and launched into a story. 'So we're Taiwanese, and my parents believe that on the seventh day after a person dies they come back for one last visit. It's a final chance to say goodbye, I guess.

'I remember we laid out all my brother's favourite food in the kitchen and opened all the doors and windows, and then sat and waited. We were supposed to sit there all night, but I was eleven! So of course I fell asleep, and I remember being woken in the middle of the night by Mum and my ama shrieking because there was a moth in the house. I mean, of course there was a moth in the house: they left all the windows and doors open. But they thought it was him, come to say goodbye.

'Then that was kind of it. We didn't really talk about him after that. It was as if he'd disappeared. Which he did,' she said sadly. 'I guess he did.'

Ev felt her eyes prickle, thinking about little Emily carrying the weight of her parents' grief. 'That must've been so hard,' she said. Do not cry on a first date, she told herself. Don't you dare cry.

'Yeah. I still get sad thinking about what he could've been, you know? Would he have been a doctor or a musician or an accountant? But you know all of this . . .'

Ev stayed quiet. In the last year, she'd often thought about the unfolded map of lives cut short: all the things he could've been and done.

'God, bleurgh.' Emily pressed her palm to her forehead. 'Listen to me prattling on. Sorry!'

'You're not prattling,' Ev said. 'Not at all. It's really nice to talk to someone who gets it, who's not scared off by it.'

'Don't worry. It's not scary. It's just . . . life,' Emily said. 'There is something to be said,' she began, and then paused, started again. 'There is a smugness that comes with grief. That comes with the knowledge grief brings. Maybe you're not there yet, maybe smugness isn't the right word.'

'No, I think I know what you mean. It's like you're the newly divorced guest at a wedding. You know something other people don't know.'

'Just how bad things can be,' Emily said with a flat, knowing smile.

'But also what's survivable,' Ev said.

'Yes,' Emily said. 'Let's cheers to that, to surviving.'

They clinked glasses, made eye contact as they did, just as the superstition told them to. Ev felt like she'd had more than enough bad luck, that it was time for things to change.

'So, you must have funny teacher stories,' Emily said, changing the subject. 'Tell me all your good ones.'

Twelve

ANNIE SAT ON THE SOFA and picked at the dirt under her fingernails.

She took an unopened envelope from the coffee table. She could tell from its thickness, from the handwritten address, that it was a card. A card that would say sorry or offer a prayer or best wishes or love. The last thing she needed was more love. She had so much of it coursing inside her that sometimes she thought she might burst. People talk about the explosion of love you feel when your baby's born but never about where it's all supposed to go when he dies. There should be a dumping station, a sludge pit.

She used the corner of the envelope to scrape the last of the dirt from under her thumbnail and placed it down on the sofa next to her.

The house ticked in the evening quiet; metal cooling, wood shifting. The air around her thick like cloud. Nearby, a fly buzzed and banged against the window. She could've got up and set it free but instead she watched it flit desperately from one side of the window to the other. Banging and banging and banging in search of freedom.

The sound of her phone ringing jolted her. It was almost dark now, somehow. She'd lost whole days like this; just sitting. Time vanishing just as he did. Her phone's screen flashed urgently: *Toorak*. She didn't answer, she let it go to voicemail, turned her phone over. She might listen to the message later, she might forget.

She looked around her. In the near-darkness she could just make out the shapes of furniture: an armchair, the kitchen bench, the dining table. She wanted to stand, to get a glass of water, to walk up the stairs, brush her teeth, get into bed. But she didn't move. She just sat as the dim room turned black, as the sharp corners and edges became impossible to discern from the air.

Thirteen

NATHAN DROVE PAST THE NETTED citrus trees and big wide lawns of the northern suburbs. It was getting dark. Inside, families were turning on their lights, were sitting down to dinner together, oblivious to the horrors of the world.

Nathan parked, turned off the engine. He looked at the small house. It glowed golden from the living room lights, the curtains not yet closed. He saw Tess moving around, her dark hair pulled up in a messy ponytail on top of her head. Ruby sat on the couch reading, her legs crossed beneath her. She was almost a teenager now. She had Tess's colouring, her freckles, but personality-wise she shone with Fran's warmth.

His sister answered when he knocked.

'It's you,' she said. She seemed surprised to see him but not unhappy. They hugged. Nathan held on longer than he normally would. 'Come in,' she said.

'Uncle Nathan!' Ruby jumped up and hugged him too; her arms reached all the way around him now. He kissed the top of her head. Her shampoo smelled like strawberry bubble gum.

'Hey,' Tess said. She dried her hands on a tea towel, placed a hand on his arm as she kissed his cheek.

He followed Fran into the kitchen, still brown and orange, still falling apart. It desperately needed to be renovated but they made do. Franny always made do.

'To what do we owe the pleasure?' Fran leaned forward, resting both arms on the tiled kitchen bench. She had Cherie's thick brown hair but with Bob's curl; a streak of grey ran along her part.

'Am I not allowed to come and see my family?'

'You can come whenever you want,' she said. 'But you don't.'

She turned without waiting for a response and filled two glasses of water from the tap.

'Let's go sit out back,' she said, handing one to him and walking down the dark hallway.

'Do you want to stay for dinner, Nath?' Tess asked as they passed her in the laundry. She was pulling Ruby's school uniform out of the washing machine.

'I don't want to be an imposition,' he said.

'Never.' Tess smiled. 'It's just spag bol, but there's heaps.'

'Okay, yeah, thank you,' he said.

He followed his sister through the screen door to the garden, trying to remember the last time they'd been there. Fran was right: they didn't drop around the way they used to. Ruby would beg to see her cousin, and the four adults would sit on the plastic chairs on the sloped concrete and watch the kids play – Ruby pointing out the vegetables in the garden, saying the names slowly so he'd remember. For weeks afterwards, he'd point to every vegetable on his plate or in the shop and say 'tatoes'. Nathan smiled at the memory. He wanted to never forget these things. There were so few of them, and they were fading quickly: the sound of his cry in the night, his bobbing, milk-drunk head, tatoes. *Tatoes*. He played his son's voice again and again in his head, as if repetition would cast it in stone, keep it in place. Somewhere nearby, the sprinkler hum of a cicada.

'So,' Fran said as they sat at the plastic garden table. 'What did they do?'

Nathan looked at her, noticed the skin crinkled near her eyes.

'Am I that transparent?' he asked, feeling a flicker of shame spark like a gas stove.

'I've known you a very long time,' she said. 'There's a special wronged-by-Bob-and-Cherie face you do.' She pulled her mouth down in an exaggerated frown, furrowed her brow, crossed her arms like a sulking teenager.

He laughed. 'Fuck off.' She looked just like him. He knew it. He hated that he was so easily read, so easily seen. He liked to think part of what made him so good at his job (what used to make him so good at his job) was that he had a poker face. And yet there were two people who could see straight through him: his sister and his wife. Probably Tess too. And Ev. Claire. Maybe everyone had been able to see exactly who he was this whole time. Maybe no one was fooled.

He put his glass of water down on the table and leaned forward, elbows on his knees.

'I went to Toorak for dinner,' he said.

'Just you?'

He nodded.

'Bob?'

He shook his head and she grimaced.

'Working or "out"?'

Their father had spent many evenings of their childhood 'out'. It could've meant wining and dining clients, being wined and dined. Mostly, they were sure, it meant he was with another woman.

Nathan shrugged. 'I don't know if she even knows anymore.'

'I feel sorry for her sometimes,' Fran said.

'After everything?' He didn't understand how someone could have a heart that big. Cherie's comment earlier, 'Our only grand-child', stung him. She and Bob refused to accept Ruby. He couldn't imagine how deep it cut for Fran and Tess.

'Do you remember Belinda?' Fran asked.

'I will never forget Belinda.' He'd spent a lot of time in his early teens thinking about her. Those tits were etched into his memory, a tongue and groove, a long-standing agreement between his hand and his dick. He wasn't smart enough back then to put two and two together, to realise that his dad was sleeping with her. A vague, sepia-tinted memory edged its way into his brain. Of seeing them in Bob's office together, all those lingering looks between them. Cherie must have known about all of it, turned a blind eye if not been complicit. They both disgusted him.

'And there was Gwen,' Fran said.

'Jenny,' Nathan said. 'Lucy.'

Fran raised her eyebrows. 'I don't think I met Lucy.'

'She was the receptionist when he made me do work experience at the firm,' Nathan said. Poor Lucy. She couldn't have been older than twenty.

Fran screwed her face up, pretended to shudder.

'So why are you here and not with Cherie?' she asked.

'I told her to go fuck herself and stormed out of the house,' he said sheepishly. 'She told me not to bring' – he put on a voice, high and tight – 'all my feelings into this.'

Fran cackled. 'Bloody hell, she's a monster,' she said. 'Do you think your reaction had anything to do with' – she paused – 'tomorrow?'

'Yes,' he said quietly. 'It had everything to do with that.'

The screen door creaked and he looked up to see Ruby standing there shyly, holding a book. Fran saw her too, motioned for her to join them. She came and stood between them. The book was a scrapbook, the cover hand-painted with a photo glued on top.

'I made this for you and Annie,' she said, passing it to him with two hands.

'We were going to drop it in tomorrow but you've saved us a trip,' Fran said.

Nathan took the book from her. The photo on the front was of their two families. Two couples, two kids, taken on his second birthday. On his last day.

'Rubes,' he said, he was already crying. 'Come here.' She took a step towards him and he hugged her. 'Thank you.'

'It's for Annie too.' She put her arm around his shoulder. 'I know that it will make you sad, but I thought one day it might make you happy too,' she said. 'It's to help you remember him.'

He made eye contact with Fran through his tears and she was welling up too. He shook his head as if to say, *This kid*, and Franny smiled as if to say, *I know*.

'Sit with me and we'll look through it together?' Nathan said, and Ruby nodded, proud. She pulled one of the plastic chairs across the concrete and put it next to him.

'I'm going to help Tess with dinner.' Fran stood, put her hand on Nathan's shoulder and squeezed it, then left them alone, the screen door bouncing in the doorjamb, then settling.

'This is from when he was in Annie's tummy.' Ruby pointed at a photo of Annie, about seven months pregnant, beaming. 'We hadn't met him yet, but we already loved him.'

Nathan felt his heart burst, but not in the bad way, not in the painful way. He felt full of love for this child, for his own.

She turned the page.

'This is from when he was born and you let me hold him in the hospital.' Ruby pointed to a photo of him swaddled in a hospital blanket, a tiny thing. Nathan remembered the first time he held him, the feeling of the tiny warm body on his bare chest, the smell of him. His impossibly small fingers, his little ears. Later, the sour smell of milky vomit on everything. The way Annie always knew exactly what to do somehow, exactly how to feed him, to soothe him, to make him laugh. It wasn't just that she'd read all the books or looked at all the blogs; it seemed instinctual in a way it wasn't for Nathan. During those late nights in the first few months he'd watch her, her face illuminated by the screen of her phone as she timed feeds, and a love he didn't know was possible would hit him like a wave. A love not just for Annie but for the family she'd made.

'I really miss him,' Ruby said.

Nathan made a noise he didn't recognise. A quaking flood of grief leaving his body.

'Me too,' Nathan said through tears. 'He loved you so much,' he said and hugged Ruby again. 'I'm going to treasure this book forever. It's the nicest thing anyone has ever given me. Thank you so much.'

'As if,' Ruby said, but she was beaming.

'Truly,' he said, and he meant it. 'Thank you.'

'Dinner's ready,' a voice called from inside.

'You go – I'll just be a minute,' Nathan said, and he watched her skip into the house.

The sound of taps and voices, of plates. A cutlery drawer stuck in its tracks, slammed shut. He clutched the book under his arm and tried to breathe. He stood, wiped his nose on his sleeve, and walked towards the warmth of the house, towards the light.

Fourteen

'TIME TO STOP WORKING.'

John Noble stood at the door of Claire's office, his cheeks already redder than usual. He was holding a beer by its neck. 'It's Friday night, for god's sake. Plus, it's not much fun celebrating someone who's not even there.'

'It was a team effort,' Claire said. Her legs ached, her back. She lifted her arms above her head and John winced as her shoulders cracked. She hadn't moved in hours. She'd reacquired the skill she'd honed in law school: the ability to ignore her humming bladder. No time to pee – only time to work.

She saved everything, took one last look at her email and shut her laptop. To her surprise it was dark outside. Her stomach rumbled. She'd learned to ignore that too.

'I guess I have time for one,' she said, and followed him down the hall to the kitchen where some associates, two managing partners and a few assistants were drinking in small clumps.

They cheered when they saw her, again when Gideon Strong popped the cork from a bottle of champagne. One thing Strong, King and Noble knew how to do well was celebrate. This time, the victory was Claire's. A client had finally signed a contract and her long-drawn negotiations had made the firm a tidy profit. Another success. These wins used to make her happy, used to make her proud. Now they felt like something happening on a TV show she had on in the background. She was just glad it was done and dusted.

Someone handed her a glass, filled it with bubbling liquid, the white froth teetering dangerously close to the lip of the glass but never going over. She watched it as it sunk back down.

'Speech! Speech!' someone yelled, and Claire realised all eyes were on her. A fork was clanged against a glass as if they were at a wedding.

She thanked each one of the associates by name, the partners, the assistants.

'This was a big win,' Claire said. 'I know a lot of you worked long hours to make it happen.' She tried to look each one of them in the eye. 'Your hard work has not gone unnoticed. Thank you. You can all go home, take the next two days off,' she joked.

'Who says we're going home?' one of the associates called, his deep voice booming, and a few of them cackled.

She knew they had a reputation for playing as hard as they worked. She heard the rumours of who out of the group ended up jammed inside toilet stalls at three in the morning snorting cocaine through rolled-up banknotes. Maybe tonight she'd go with them. Maybe tonight she'd let loose.

'Come with me,' John said. 'I want to show you something.'

Claire expected it was a contract, something for her to cast her eyes over, an email he wanted her opinion on. But he led her down the carpeted hall, past the toilets to the service elevator. It came fast; it wouldn't be in demand until about five the next morning, when deliveries started arriving for the cafes downstairs. Claire had witnessed the workings of the building at all hours. She knew the names of the night security guards' children, asked after them often.

'Don't look so worried,' John said as the lift doors closed.

It smelled musty in there, like a place she wasn't meant to be.

'I'm pretty sure this is how people are disappeared in a John Grisham novel,' she said, trying to rearrange her face, to loosen her lips, relax her jaw.

'Far too many cameras,' John Noble said with a speed that alarmed Claire.

As the lift doors opened on an upper floor, he launched himself forward, his long legs, his lurching walk. He pulled a key ring from his pocket, unlocked an unmarked door and held it open for her to pass through.

He took the stairs two steps at a time. He was slightly out of breath when they got to the top. The key again. He opened another door.

In front of them vents pummelled steam into the sky. The wind picked up and flapped the lapels of her suit jacket. Claire stepped forward. Out past the vents, over railing that ran around the top of the building, was the sparkling city, was the night sky.

'Whoa,' she said. 'I thought we weren't allowed up here?'

'We're not.' John smiled and walked closer to the edge, pulling a packet of cigarettes from the inside pocket of his jacket. She followed him, stood beside him against the railing.

'I am going to assume you're one of those perfect people with no vices,' he said and lit the cigarette, the flame burning strong, hot, bright.

'Far from perfect,' she said, and took the packet off him and pretended to throw it over the edge.

'Don't!' He grabbed for them and she smiled, handing them back. 'It's my last packet and then I'm quitting,' he said. 'This time I really mean it.'

'Sure,' she said. 'Sure.' She turned to look in the other direction. Between the other skyscrapers she could just make out the black oil smudge of the bay. She wondered if she and John Noble were the only people up this high. Just them and the birds. Them and the bats. And the clouds and the sky and the stars.

John took a deep drag. Claire leaned over, took the cigarette off him, put it to her mouth, sucked in the white smoke.

'Atta girl,' he said as she coughed. The nicotine made her dizzy.

'Disgusting,' she said, swallowing hard, passing it back. 'So why are we up here?'

In the five years she'd worked for him, John Noble had never invited her for a social chat.

'I wanted you to see the view before you leave us,' he said, still facing the night sky.

'I . . .' she began, flummoxed. 'I'm not . . .'

'But you're thinking about it?' he asked, turning to face her now. 'It's a landmark case, what Helen's doing. A career making class action. You'd be crazy not to think about it.'

'How?' She hadn't even looked at the offer yet. How did he know?

'I know people,' he said. 'I have spies everywhere.'

He paused. Around them the hum of the building, all the things it needed in order to keep running, keep working.

'I won't hold it against you if you go,' he added. 'But maybe you should think about what it is you're leaving.'

Claire felt the wind pick up; it blew her hair across her face. She hoped that would be enough of a mask to cover her shock. She felt not exposed, but seen. She hated it.

'I . . .' She tried to speak. Couldn't. She wondered what else he knew. If he knew she was itching to run away. That it was the only thing she knew how to do when things felt this bad, this hard. So broken they were unfixable. He kept going, didn't make her continue.

'You're on a good track here, Claire – you know that, right? There's a clear route to the top. You've worked hard, you're smart. The clients love you. We'd support you if you wanted to' – he waved his hand with a sort of dismissive indifference – 'have a baby or something. Do whatever you need to do.'

John didn't bother finishing his cigarette. He stubbed it out on the scratched metal railing.

'Think about it,' he said, and chucked the butt over the edge. 'The doors aren't locked from this side.' He walked off without her.

She watched him go. She turned and stood on her tiptoes to look over the side of the building. A metre below was a strip of concrete covered in cigarette butts, another railing. To stop people falling, she imagined; to save them if they jumped. Far below that, the road. It seemed to shimmer with light and movement, with wind and distance and space. She thought about all the layers of things between her and the dirt.

She'd explained this to Al on their first date. That she thought the whole world was just made up of things, layers of things on other things. He'd looked around the dimly lit pub, its walls adorned with manufactured kitsch, and laughed. There wasn't a thing in there he could find to disprove her theory. The pizza between them, the table, the carpet, the floorboards, foundations, pipes and cables.

'What else you got?' Al asked, and leaned forward a little, just enough for the space between them to change.

Did it count as running away if the opportunity came to you? She was following. She was following Helen Parkinson, she was following her dream.

She circled the roof, walking along the railing as far as she could in one direction, then doubling back, looking at the view from each angle, taking it in. Seeing everything from up high reminded her of the trip she'd taken to Europe with Al. Both of them taking a month off to sit on beaches and read trashy crime novels (her) while Al lugged that one same copy of *War and Peace* he'd never finish from Airbnb to Airbnb, taking up space in the beach bag that was otherwise used for cans of local beer sweating in the heat, for bread and cheese and cold cuts of meat and local tomatoes that popped with ripeness. In big cities, they always climbed the highest things to look at views. The Duomo in Florence, the Eiffel Tower. All these cities seen from above. She thought back to their week in Croatia, too.

•

IT WAS THE last leg of the trip. A few days in Zagreb first – a mistake, they'd decided, as the city streets sweltered, the nearest beach too far away – and then a bus to Pula, where Claire stood on the street, the slip of paper in her hand with an address. The handwriting was hard to read and maybe it was misspelled, but this must've been it. Seven Kovačićeva ulica. The combination of the letters confused her brain, made her feel cross-eyed, something it pained her to admit to Al, this man who would not stop taking photos of her, this man who was fluent in two languages.

The house that used to stand there had been described to her in flashes.

'Stone house, big stone house,' Dida used to say. Cabbage braising on the stove, fish caught from the rocks being gutted in the sink. Cigarette smoke. A high wall. In the garden, a fig tree, a lemon tree. Always the smell of cooking. A red front door. They would hide from the sounds of the war in the cellar. Damp and cold and scared.

As she got older, he'd talk about the long walk to Trieste, a hostel for refugees. Then waiting and waiting for sixteen months with nothing to do. She remembered a day at the beach with her family, the long yellow sand, her grandfather shirtless. She was embarrassed back then by his tanned leathery skin, by the wiry white hairs on his chest, by the volume at which he'd speak, how he'd order her mum around, order Claire around, sneak beer to her brother, never her. He'd never go near the water; he'd just sit in a low chair and watch, smoke, complain. 'Imagine this for twenty hours in the canal.' He pointed at the sand. 'From a ship, desert everywhere, nothing but sand. *Suez*. More like sewer,' he said with two winks and a sharp elbow, then he laughed until he coughed.

He told her once about the storms in the Indian Ocean, the sea so rough that everything smelled of vomit. He swore he saw people's faces turn green. She'd screwed her nose up; baulked at the stories he'd told her about hardship. She'd been too scared to ask what was so bad that they had to walk for twenty-four hours and cross a border under the cover of darkness to escape it. She knew that once in Italy, they waited for news of the ship to take them to Australia, with no idea what was in store for them, no idea if it was all worth it. But she'd never asked was worth running away from, what was worth staying for. Her only takeaway was that running away was sometimes the only option.

In Pula with Al, she wanted to find the house Dida had described to her. The house of his childhood. If they were on the right street, in the right spot, the house was long gone. Instead she found an apartment block. Grey with a newish lick of baby-pink paint along the front wall. There was no lemon tree, no fig tree, nothing left to feel nostalgic about. All of that disappeared after he left his home town in pursuit of a new life and, later, when he died in his sleep.

'Am I supposed to feel something?' she asked Al as he took a few photos of her in front of the apartment block to send to her dad. He took a few more photos of the block without her in them, some of the houses opposite, of the trees that could've been here when her grandfather was. She didn't know how to assess the age of a tree save for cutting it down and counting its rings.

'A fulfilment of duty, maybe. A relinquishing of obligation?' The latter he said dramatically, with a wave of his hand, as if he were shooing away all her bad feelings, her guilt, her apathy.

'I should've cared more when he was alive. He tried to tell me stories. I just wasn't interested.' The shame covered her like a shroud.

'Weren't you thirteen when he died?' Al asked.

'Still,' she said.

'And didn't he also take you with him to loan sharks and dodgy pokies joints?'

Claire shrugged.

They walked back through the streets to the old part of town, past cracked and graffitied walls. On one, *No Nazis* was spray-painted in red.

'I like it here,' Al said, pretending to pose next to it with two thumbs up. Claire smiled at him, kept walking, so he had to jog slightly to catch up.

They ate overpriced pizza in an old square, their Cokes circled by European wasps, bright yellow bodies always in search of something. Never settled, never satisfied.

'This is the Temple of Augustus,' Al read from the guidebook after they'd paid the bill, after they'd planned their afternoon around the top five things a travel blog had told them to do. 'It was probably built as a tribute to the emperor sometime between 27BC and his death in 14AD.'

'Pretty old,' Claire said, standing on the temple's steps. She could feel the cool dark air inside.

'It was built on a podium. The columns are Corinthian blah blah blah . . . Oh, this is interesting: it was almost totally destroyed by a bomb during an Allied air raid in 1944, then reconstructed in 1947.'

They both looked up at it, searching for cracks or signs of its near destruction. It looked sturdy. Faultless.

DAYS LATER, AFTER an hour-long bus ride north, a bike ride south along the coast, Claire waded into a turquoise sea. Across the water was the hilltop spire and the tangled stone houses of Rovinj. A jumble of terracotta-tiled roofs and morbid histories. She thought about her grandparents, she thought about the Temple of Augustus, admired all the things it was possible to survive. Al was under water already. He surfaced next to her and wrapped his long arms around her, pulling her against the wet of his bare chest, his skin darker with the sun. She let him pull her down with him, down under the water. She closed her eyes, held her breath. She'd go anywhere with him.

•

FOR A LONG time, Claire had kept a picture of Al as the lock screen on her phone. Shirtless, on that narrow sandy beach in Croatia, the sky wide and blue, the grin on his face pure happiness, real happiness. A streak of sunscreen not quite rubbed in across his big, beautiful nose. His lips parted to reveal large straight teeth that just came out that way, no braces, no cavities. She can't remember exactly when she changed the picture on her screen. At some point in the last year, when seeing him happy hurt too much. Now it was the furry rug of Crunchie's ginger tummy that greeted her whenever she looked at her phone. It was Crunchie's ginger tummy that stood between her and news about the job, about her new life in Sydney. She wondered how long Helen would wait for her. She wondered how they'd stuck the Temple of Augustus back together, how much time it took, what kind of glue.

The wind picked up, a rough gust from across the bay, and it pushed her lightly against the railing. She imagined going over, landing on the studded carpet of cigarettes butts. Or worse. She shivered, then walked back to the door, turning to take one last look at the city from up here, one last look at the sky.

Fifteen

CARS RUSHED BY. THE SUN was gone but the sky was still striped with pink, dark blue. Al didn't understand how those colours blended into one another. He didn't understand how anything worked. Above him, a few bats flapped menacingly across the sky in search of food. The silhouettes of the palm trees made him feel like he was somewhere else. He thought of the thick date palms he'd seen in Ahvaz. Home, technically, but not. He'd only been to Iran once, age fifteen. All spots and greasy hair. All he'd wanted to do was listen to the Beastie Boys on his Discman, not sit politely in the homes of distant relatives he didn't know. Relatives who looked at him with a mix of pity and shame.

It felt too early to go home, even though he knew Crunchie would be there waiting, hungry, angry that no one had fed her yet. If he went home, she would eat quickly, sulk for a few minutes and then strut across the sofa to his lap, where she'd sit on the keyboard if he was on his laptop or chew the edge of whatever book he was reading until he gave her his undivided attention.

Go home and feed the cat, he told himself. Watch a show. Do not search the Woodwards, do not search Carmen's name. Make an appointment with your doctor, get a referral to a therapist. Go home, he willed himself. Go home. Above, he saw a twinkle of what could've been a meteor but was probably a plane. Go home. But the thought of being there alone made him fizz with anxiety. All the empty hours still ahead of him to think and worry, to sink further. Claire wouldn't be back until late, when she'd silently slip into bed beside him, and he wouldn't realise she was there until she or Crunchie woke him the following morning.

She worked so much now. Six days a week, fourteen hours a day. Before, she'd apologise for it. Claim it was a means to an end. That she was getting to a point where she'd have more autonomy, more control, more money. Now she embraced it, she plunged headlong into it. Like she was grateful for the distraction, the escape.

They both pretended it wasn't obvious what they were trying to hide from. From those few minutes that changed them both.

He pulled his phone out of his back pocket. No new messages. No one was thinking about him, no one was worried. He should text Katrina and claim he'd left the meeting to throw up. Tell her he had gastro. No one ever questioned diarrhoea.

Al felt sober now; the food, the fresh air were doing him good. But with sobriety came the niggling feeling that there was a reason Claire hadn't been in touch. His heart clenched. He imagined her falling: on the grass, her neck broken, blood pooling on the ground where she'd hit her head. He imagined her on wooden floorboards. Lying on her back. Not breathing. Her lips blue. A faint heartbeat but her blood, her brain, deprived of oxygen for too long. Nathan screaming, Annie crying. Ev trying to clear the airway. Al on the phone to triple-O saying hurry, hurry. All of it too little, too late.

IT WAS NINE thirty by the time he reached the strip of shops. He'd started thinking and the thinking kept him walking. He wished again for his headphones; for music or a podcast to drown out his thoughts. But paying attention to the traffic, to the sky, it helped.

The restaurants were busy. Clinking glasses and cutlery on plates. The low chatter of friends, of couples on dates. A man was busking outside Piedimonte's: a slow, folksy rendition of 'Wonderwall' that reignited Al's anger with a crackle, as if two flints were sparking against one another.

He hated these suburbs. Fully gentrified. Packed full of rich white people. Buskers who thought it was okay to sing 'Wonderwall', for fuck's sake.

He wasn't sure why he'd walked down here. There were bars near his house. An old pub with sticky carpet where he could've slunk in for one then gone home. But here he was, in a suburb he'd tried to avoid for the last year. The suburb where Annie and Nathan lived. The suburb where it had happened. Five hundred metres from Nathan and Annie's house. Coming here magnified his feelings of loss. He couldn't think about the one death without thinking about the other. His grief for the two kids he'd loved braided together forever.

He needed a drink.

Al had just passed the busker – crooning his way into the long, nasal chorus – when he spotted a familiar figure up ahead. A gait that was both confident and somehow skulking. It was Nathan. Of course, of course, it was Nathan.

'Shit,' Al whispered and slipped off course, sideways, through the sliding doors of the supermarket.

It didn't occur to him until he was halfway down the pasta aisle, swimming in that bright fluorescent supermarket light, that this was probably Nathan's destination too. That if Nathan hadn't seen him out on the street, he'd almost certainly see him in here.

He strode past the sauces and along the ends of the aisles, where there were stacks of sardine tins and almost-out-of-date packets of ladyfingers on special.

He turned left at the meat fridges and ended up among the dairy products. If he doesn't see me, I'll just go home, Al told himself. Classic bargaining. He'd done it before. If you just bring her back. If you just bring him back. I'll be good. I'll be better. I'll drink less. I'll visit Dad.

He stood with his back to the aisle, pretending to be perusing the cheeses and yoghurts.

He didn't even know why he'd run, why he'd panicked. Maybe because the last time he'd seen Nathan and Annie it had been so awkward. So sad. He and Claire had gone over for a cup of tea. They'd taken cake. Was it someone's birthday? When had that been? He counted back. It wasn't last month. It could've been Annie's birthday in late September. Time had lost all its meaning. Somehow it was November again. Somehow he had all the feelings of the year two thousand again. The same grief. The same despair. The same anger.

That day they'd mostly exchanged work stories, talked about Crunchie, every so often falling into a heavy silence, into a fogged sadness. He wondered if, in those silences, Annie and Nathan were blaming him. If they were seething inside. If they wished him ill – worse, wished him gone. After an hour, Claire had made an excuse for them to leave and they'd been silent on the tram home. Al had found it exhausting, the juggling of all these feelings. It felt like a full-time job.

He'd taken a beer to bed with him when they got home that afternoon, napped for an hour while Claire worked at the kitchen table, while Crunchie stared out the front window. He envied her life, the simplicity of it. That she slept, chased bugs, was fed on demand. No responsibilities, no blame, no regret. Even when she sat on his bedside table and knocked things off one by one, Crunchie felt no guilt.

He thought of Claire again. He wanted to call her. He wanted to get out of the fucking dairy section of this supermarket. He turned to find Nathan in front of him.

'I thought that was you,' Nathan said, a hand on Al's shoulder there in the bright supermarket lights.

'Oh, hey, mate,' Al said.

Nathan stood there, unflinching, unmoving, unwavering. Nathan was tall but not quite Al tall. His broad sporting physique nothing on Al's heft. They must've looked strange, these two huge men standing silently in the dairy aisle, searching for words.

'You in a hurry to get some yoghurt or something?' Nathan said, putting him out of his misery.

'Something like that,' Al said. How was he supposed to explain it?

'I saw you,' Nathan said. 'I saw you duck in here when you saw me.'

'No.' Al felt his face burn, his guts stretch out inside him like mozzarella on TV pizza. 'See you?' He couldn't even get a full sentence out. He wanted the ground to swallow him up.

'It's just me,' Nathan said, squeezing Al's arm through his denim jacket, through his t-shirt. 'It's just me.'

Al felt his shoulders loosen, felt himself calm, felt himself steady in Nathan's grip there in the dairy aisle, the two of them hanging on for dear life among the almond milk, among the soy.

Sixteen

NATHAN FOLLOWED AL INTO THE bar a few doors down from Piedimonte's. The place was bustling, full of life. They slid into a recently vacated booth, empty glasses still on the table, and sat diagonally across from one another, the narrow space a tight squeeze for their long legs. Al bought them a pint each. The condensation dripped down the outside of each glass making small round pools on the wood between them.

'I tried to punch my cousin tonight,' Al said bashfully, a big hand around his pint glass.

'Which cousin?' Nathan asked, worrying for a second, just a second.

'Oh god, Javeed, of course – Javeed.' Al looked mortified.

'What happened?'

'He was being a shit,' Al muttered. 'But I was prickly before I got there.'

They stayed quiet while a man lit the candle between them, cleared the empty glasses.

'I'm really sorry I did that before,' Al continued, the flame flickering in the low light. Nathan watched him trying to get the words out. 'It was shitty.' A beat. 'Really shitty.'

'It's okay,' Nathan said. 'I don't always want to be around myself either.' He smiled to indicate to Al that he was joking. Mostly joking.

'Do you ever feel like it just doesn't stop? That life is just one shit thing after another?'

'Tell me about it,' Nathan said, and he took a drink and he liked the way the drink made him feel. He wondered if drinking more in the last year would've made things better. If being out in the world would've helped. Surrounded by life. Surrounded by people who didn't know what had happened.

'Yeah, sorry, of course you do.' Al shook his head, doing that thing people did when you were the bereaved, the hardest done by.

'No, I meant tell me about it. Tell me what's on your mind, what's going on.' Nathan leaned forward to show he was ready.

'Are you sure?'

'Positive,' he said. 'Take my mind off my own stuff for a bit.'

'Well, it's partly to do with your stuff too but okay,' Al said tentatively. 'We can stop at any point.'

'Do we need a safe word?' Nathan asked, and Al smiled.

Al traced the pattern of a droplet down the edge of his glass with his finger. 'Okay,' he began. 'I don't really talk about this much.' He took a deep breath. 'On New Year's Eve in 1999 we had a party and there was an accident, and my friend – she died.'

'Jesus,' Nathan said.

He thought back to his own New Year's Eve that year. A drunken party at the family beach house, a midnight swim with Annie. It was a perfect night. Back then, it would never have occurred to him that anyone else's night could be going any differently; back then, he and Annie were the centre of the universe. Now he was more aware than ever that there are bad things happening all the time.

'Her name was Carmen. I loved her, I think.' Nathan heard Al's voice quiver a little when he said it. 'She was beautiful and did a great Lisa Simpson impression and had a laugh like an outboard motor.' Al smiled a sad smile, tears forming in his eyes.

'What happened?'

'She slipped and fell off a roof. It was just a dumb accident.'

Nathan felt the pang of familiarity. The anger at a life cut short. He thought of her parents. The cops showing up, a phone call in the night. They were part of the same club now. The very worst one in the world.

'Here's the thing, though,' Al went on. 'I feel like there's always a chain of events, you know. All these cogs in the wheel of . . . death.'

'That makes it sound like a medieval torture device,' Nathan said.

'It is, I guess. A psychological torture device, because if you were any way involved or present or just – fuck, I don't know what I'm trying to say except that it's hard not to feel . . . implicated.'

'So you feel guilty that this girl . . .'

'Carmen.'

'Right, you feel guilty that Carmen died because you were at a party almost twenty years ago?'

'Not just that. I brought drugs.' Al pulled at the short hair of his beard. 'I brought some ecstasy to the party.'

'And she took some?'

'No,' Al said. 'But her boyfriend did, and he was up there with her.'

Nathan didn't understand, couldn't see the threads Al had strung between pieces of evidence in his mind. He sat quietly, waiting for Al to elaborate.

'He convinced her to go up there with him. If he hadn't taken it, maybe he wouldn't have. Maybe he'd have caught her before she fell? I don't know.'

'So you feel guilty for something that had nothing to do with you except that you were roughly in the vicinity when it happened.'

'You're starting to sound like Zahra. It's just a hard feeling to shake.' Al hesitated for a second. 'Especially when it's happened more than once.'

'You had more than one friend die?' Nathan was confused.

Al didn't say anything. He just sat there. Nathan could tell he was waiting for him to work something out, put two and two together. The beer had made his head feel cloudy.

Al took another deep breath. 'It's just, it's not . . .'

A couple sat down in the booth behind theirs. Nathan felt his seat move with the weight of their backs.

'It's not the only party I've brought drugs to where someone's . . .' Al nodded as if his head was typing out Morse code, as if Nathan should be able to finish the sentence. As if that was enough to go on. 'Someone's' – Al stopped; Nathan wanted to reach across the table and squeeze the words out of him – 'died.'

Nathan thought for a minute, then it dawned on him, and his eyes welled up with tears. There was no time to stop them.

'Wait,' Nathan said. 'Wait.'

Al looked down at his lap. He wouldn't look up.

Nathan whispered the next words in case anyone could hear them over the music: 'The joint?'

'Yeah,' Al said. He looked sweaty, stricken with guilt.

'Al, no,' Nathan said. 'No. No no no no no no. What happened had nothing to do with that.'

'But it's the butterfly effect, the cogs,' Al said.

Al had been torturing himself for a whole year, Nathan realised. For almost twenty years.

'No,' Nathan said again. 'I can't let you feel bad about that. I can't.' The tears came now, flowing down Nathan's cheeks. 'Please don't tell me you've been feeling guilty about that?'

'If I hadn't . . . brought it . . . then . . .' Al shrugged.

'Yeah, but if I hadn't taken that call, if I hadn't gone upstairs . . . If I hadn't sat at my desk for five minutes and looked at my emails. If I'd gone straight downstairs, I could've caught him before he ate it and taken him back to bed. I could've found him while he was still breathing.' Nathan paused to take a breath. He hadn't said any of this out loud before, never vocalised the chain of events he felt he'd started, the weight he too carried. 'Al, this isn't your fault.'

'It's not your fault either,' Al said.

'I know. It's not my fault. It's not Annie's fault. It's not Ev's fault, though god knows she blamed herself for a while too.'

'Ev?' Al asked. He was crying too now. Nathan wondered how the two of them must look to everyone else in the bar.

'If she hadn't put any marshmallows in those lolly bags,' Nathan said. He hadn't said this out loud before either, but at the beginning he thought it. He wanted to blame Ev too. Those fucking marshmallows. Now he just thanked god she kept showing up. He didn't know what they'd have done without her.

'I've thought of every single what if, every single one. And it doesn't change anything. It doesn't do any good. It doesn't bring him back.'

'I know,' Al said. He was swaying slightly, as if the grief had made him drunk. 'I wish I could do something to bring him back.'

'Me too, mate,' Nathan said. 'Fuck, I'd give anything.' His breathing was staccato through tears. 'Please,' he said, 'please know that none of it is your fault. You need to let it go. Let yourself be free.'

And suddenly Al was laughing.

'Sorry,' Al said. 'Get a listen of yourself. *Let yourself be free.*' He laughed hard, his enormous body doubling over, his hair getting too close to the flame of the candle. Nathan moved it out of the way, then he started to laugh too.

'What's happened to me?' Nathan caught his breath finally; Al too. Both of them breathing hard, both of them a mess of tears and snot and bone-deep exhaustion.

He picked up his empty pint glass and wiggled it. Al nodded, lifted his legs so Nathan could slide out.

Nathan leaned against the long wooden bar, squeezed between two sets of friends on bar stools. He ordered, watched the liquid fizz and froth in the glasses, one after the other. He glanced back at his friend, who sat picking wax off the candle, head down. He imagined Al at eighteen, too tall for his own good, carrying around all this guilt, doubling down on it a year ago. How was he still standing?

Nathan had met Al for the first time at the Union. Claire had introduced Al to Ev already, of course. Nathan sometimes felt jealous of the closeness of Claire and Ev's friendship. Although the three of them had met at exactly the same time back at uni, Claire and Ev shared something different.

Al had got to the pub first and was sitting alone when Nathan arrived. He'd amassed a collection of extra chairs, seemingly unsure about the exact size of the group he was meeting. When Nathan walked in, he saw how nervous Al was, looking at the door anxiously every time it opened, so he went straight to the bar and bought two pints. By the time Annie arrived they were two drinks in and felt like old friends. Claire got there last, not flustered by her lateness. She kissed Al's cheek then made her way around the table saying hello to everyone. She pulled up a chair next to Al.

'Sorry,' she said again. 'One of those days.'

'It was actually nice getting to know Al without you here,' Annie said. She was drinking chardonnay, and it always made her quite drunk very quickly. Annie nicked a giant chip out of Al's bowl and ate it in tiny bites with her mouth open, blowing on it to cool it down.

'Maybe for you,' Al said and put his arm around the back of Claire's chair, his hand on her shoulder. Nathan looked at Ev watching them. She must've felt a pang of jealousy: Claire had spent only five minutes on Tinder, swiped right on exactly one person, and here he was.

They stayed until closing, Al fitting in so easily it was as if he'd always been there. Nathan remembered feeling warmed by the fire, warmed by the company of his friends. Happy: plain and simple happy.

Now these people he loved felt like strangers going through the motions and obligations of friendship. All five of them carrying different sides of something heavy.

Nathan put the two pints on the table and slid back into the booth. Someone had turned the music up.

'What are you doing out, anyway?' Al asked.

'I went to see my parents.'

'Oh.' Al nodded, raised his eyebrows to indicate, *Say no more.*

'We were meant to have dinner, but I ended up yelling at Cherie and storming out instead.'

'Sounds like a fun night,' Al said and took a big gulp of his beer. A pause between them was punctured by the sound of laughter from a nearby table.

'Aaaargh,' Nathan said. He sank down in the seat, his legs banging against the opposite bench. 'It's fucked that we're supposed to just keep going. Like all these awful things happen and what, we just keep listening to podcasts and paying our taxes?'

Al smiled a sad smile.

'He would've been three tomorrow,' he continued. 'Three.' Nathan tried to think about his second birthday party. There'd been so much colour that day: a three-tiered rainbow cake, balloons. But his thoughts about the birthday party were always replaced quickly by the bright lights of the hospital waiting room.

The corner they sat in quietly for what felt like weeks, Annie's head in his lap as she cried.

'Do you think we should do something tomorrow?' he asked.

'Maybe it would help,' Al said hopefully.

Nathan looked around the bar. It was full now, the music almost too loud for them to hear each other without yelling. Everyone looked young, carefree, unburdened. Nathan felt old, encumbered. There was a couple sitting at the bar who couldn't keep their hands off each other, him kissing her neck while she was trying to talk, their hands on each other's legs. They had nothing to worry about but their desire for each other. They hadn't lost anything yet.

'I'll talk to Annie about it,' he said eventually. He looked down at his watch. 'Shit, it's after eleven. I need to go.' He drained the last of his pint.

'Me too,' Al said. 'Crunch needs her dinner – she'll be livid.'

They both slid sideways out of the booth, and Nathan led the way through the crowd that bottlenecked by the bar, through the glass door, onto the street. They stood awkwardly, too close together.

'I'm glad we did this,' Al said.

'Me too. Promise me we'll do it more often. No more chasing you down the dairy aisle.'

'Promise,' Al said. 'Tomorrow?'

'I'll let you know,' Nathan said. 'And I'm sorry about your friend. About Carmen. About everything.'

Al put his hand out as if to shake, but Nathan pulled him in for a hug. They held each other. They didn't slap each other's backs; they stood still, their bodies pressed together. When they finally pulled away, Nathan wiped his eyes.

A tram approached. Nathan pointed to it and Al waved as he started jogging up the street to the stop. The tram was slowed by traffic, Al assisted by the length of his legs. Nathan watched him climb up the steps, watched the tram trundle off up St Georges Road.

Nathan walked back to where he'd parked. His plan had been to buy Annie flowers from the supermarket, but it was too late now. Through the glass doors he could see the lights were off, the registers closed down for the night.

He unlocked the car, the doors clicked, the lights flashed twice. He'd only had two pints; he'd be fine to drive. He looked up and out at the sky, at the fingernail of a moon up there. A little sliver of another world. A bright glow behind smoke-coloured clouds.

He thought about this time last year, and how he'd worked late while Annie put together some last-minute things for the party. How he'd kissed his son goodnight. Was that the last time he'd kissed him? Had he kissed him good morning, happy birthday, just because? He wished he could remember every kiss, every hug, every word, every breath his son took, the sound of his body moving around in the world. He didn't know it was possible to miss the noises a body makes purely by being alive.

Nathan sat in the driver's seat, started the car. The gentle hum of the engine soothed him. He switched his lights on, he indicated, steered the car out into a gap in the traffic, stopped at the lights and waited as they turned from red to green.

Seventeen

EV LEFT HER BIKE IN the hall by the front door, leaning it up against the wall that was covered in black scuffs from all the other nights she'd ridden home drunk and/or needed a wee so desperately that when she got through the door she'd had to chuck her bike and run.

She'd ridden home quickly, fuelled by four wines and a quick kiss on the lips goodbye. It had been a good date, she thought. The comfortable conversation, the inside jokes they'd already started forming, Emily's easy laugh. This was how it was meant to feel. Now she looked around her flat, wide-eyed in the night-time quiet.

Her body was tired but her mind wouldn't stop buzzing. There was no way she'd get to sleep.

She got her laptop from where she'd left it on the bed, lay on the sofa with it resting on her stomach. She skipped forward a season to when Stabler was gone. Benson's hair was different, changing with the trends. She wondered what it would be like to have people to do your hair and make-up for you, to tell you how to dress and how to look, how to be. It sounded pretty good actually. To show up to work every day and pretend to be someone else. Though now that she thought about it, she supposed she'd done it before.

•

FOR TWO YEARS after law school, Ev had gone into those offices and pretended she cared, pretended that she hadn't made a huge mistake, pretended she didn't feel as though she was drowning. She'd see Nathan and Claire on the weekends and listen to them talk about their jobs, their cases, their clients, the moment when something cracked open and they saw the way forward, saw the path through. Both of them so excited by it, so alive. It wasn't like that for her.

The job itself was easy for Ev: the research, the precedents, finding the angles. But the work never satisfied her, never gave her a sense of pride. What was in it for her? Other than the monthly pay cheques that were more than she could've imagined. She'd invest all that time in the merger between blah blah and whosiwhatsit, just to make rich people richer. All through law school, she'd thought the promise of a decent pay cheque would be enough to make the job interesting, that in the real world it would all fall into place. But it didn't.

At first she thought she hated it just because it was new. That it felt like such a slog because she was a grad. In a few years, she'd have more say in the clients she worked with, she'd make even more money. Maybe then it'd feel worth it? But by year two, she was leaving the office on Friday with so much dread about coming back on Monday that she'd go home, lie down and barely move all weekend.

'You hate it, don't you?' Claire asked her one night. 'You can tell me.'

Ev was shocked. She didn't think Claire had noticed; she'd forgotten that Claire noticed everything.

'Is it that obvious?' Ev asked, resting her head in her hands. It was a Tuesday, and Ev had texted Claire from the toilets at work, asked to meet for a drink as soon as possible. Now they were sitting at a bar with big glasses of wine.

'To me it is,' Claire said. 'Nath has noticed too.' She paused. 'You just haven't been yourself lately. It's like your personality has disappeared.'

Ev felt herself grimace.

'Maybe you should change firms. I know Tranthom is hiring. What about in-house counsel?'

'I don't think that will help.' Ev sighed. 'The problem is, I just don't give a fuck about practising law – not one iota of a fuck. I didn't mind studying it but the reality of it is hell.' It felt like a relief to finally say it out loud.

Claire smiled, and reached into her bag hanging from a hook beneath the bar's lip. She opened the Moleskine notebook she was never without, pulled out the expensive pen her dad had given her as a graduation present. It cost more than a pen should, cost more than he could really afford, but he was so proud of her and wanted to show it. A pen was what he thought you bought someone who had just graduated law school. Claire would never say it, but Ev knew she cherished it. That after Al and Crunchie, it'd be the first thing she'd save in a fire.

'Okay, let's work out what you do give a fuck about then,' Claire said.

Ev took a sip of wine as Claire started writing a list of Ev's skills and qualities ('perceptive, empathetic, good general knowledge, passionate, inspiring, analytical, patient, very beautiful, amazing hair, great rack').

'Keep going, this is making me feel better,' Ev said, laughing.

By the time they'd finished their second wine, Claire had a list of potential new careers laid out in front of them. Nurse. Politician. ('I want the ability to fuck up every so often without the consequence being death or public humiliation,' Ev said in rebuttal. 'You never fuck up,' Claire said, crossing out nurse, crossing out politician.) Teacher. What was left on the list was teacher.

'You'd make a great teacher, a truly great one,' Claire said, circling the option a few times. She tore the paper from her notebook, folded it into four, handed it to Ev. 'Sit with it. See how you feel. You could do the M Teach at Melbourne and be done and working in two years.'

A teacher. It had crossed Ev's mind briefly back at school. She'd had one really good one: Ms Cockburn. You knew she really loved being a teacher, that she was dedicated; you'd have to be with a surname like that at a public high school. Ev'd had some shit teachers, too. Ones that too quickly put some of her classmates into the too-hard basket, who always seemed like they were phoning it in.

By the time Ev had cycled home that night, Claire had emailed her a course brochure, a list of deadlines and requirements. A teacher. Ms Greene. She liked the way it sounded.

•

ON SCREEN, THE credits rolled on another episode and Ev shifted herself on the couch, lifted her phone from the floor. She scrolled back and found her last message to Claire, a screen grab from Hinge. In it, you could see a man with bleached blond hair holding a machine gun, his politics listed as 'Conservative'. Ev had sent it with a screaming face emoji, Claire had reacted with a thumbs-down. She'd been distant lately; these last few months. Working too much. The last time Ev had seen her – not for want of trying – was a few weeks ago. Claire had done it before: buried herself in work. When Claire had ended things with Ed, Ev had dreams of being someone's priority, someone's someone, and of Claire being just hers for a while. She imagined the two of them would go out dancing together, but in the end she hardly saw Claire. And then Al came along. Somehow, while working too hard, Claire had also managed to meet the love of her life. Claire managed everything.

Ev started to type a message:

You okay?

She deleted it. Started another:

Miss you!

Then:

Should we organise something tomorrow?

She deleted them all and was about to put her phone down when it vibrated. A message from the unknown number:

I had a lovely time tonight. Let's do it again soon? X

Ev saved the number, put her phone down on her chest, smiled. She took a deep breath and started constructing her reply.

Eighteen

'MY SON.' ANNIE BRUSHED HER teeth while she listened to the message. Cherie's voice was tremulous. 'He yelled at me like an animal.' Quietly, wounded, Cherie muttered: 'So disrespectful.'

Annie spat, the toothpaste pink, mixed with her blood. Her gums had started bleeding six months ago. The dentist told her long periods of stress could lower the immune system, lead to inflammation. She'd cried as she lay supine in the dentist's chair, her mouth wide open, gaping. Tears wet her hair, pooled in her ears.

Annie deleted the message, deleted messages from her own mother, from her sister, ignored her twenty-two unread texts. She rinsed her mouth out with Listerine, switched off the light. She realised she'd forgotten to eat again but it was too late now. There was no hunger in her to appease. There was nothing.

In bed: a temazepam washed down with a sip of water. She should've taken it half an hour ago so she didn't have to lie in wait for the deep chemical sleep to carry her away. Now she had time in the dark to think. Time where she had to try not to feel how much she missed him, try not to run through the long list of all the things she could've done differently to stop it from happening, to stop him from dying.

She turned onto her side. The room was too hot, too stuffy. She was tired. *So tired.* And yet. She cocked a leg out from under the duvet and tried to get her brain to stop ping-ponging from one horror to the next.

She thought of the smell of his hair, of the warm weight of his body asleep in her arms. A tear slid from her eyes to the pillow, then another, another until she finally slept.

Nineteen

'WHAT'S THAT? A FUR COAT?' Janine said when she saw the picture on Claire's phone screen. She'd squeezed into the seat next to her and spent fifteen minutes yelling at Claire about how her fiancé was refusing to help organise the wedding.

'I don't trust his taste anyway, but it's the principle,' she complained.

Claire had pressed her phone to look at the time. Two in the morning already, somehow. November third already. The date hit her like a rubber mallet on a game of Whac-A-Mole. This time last year she was asleep, she thought. This time last year, she didn't know that everything was about to be unspooled like a ball of wool, like a pulled thread.

'It's my cat's fur,' Claire said, locking her phone quickly as she remembered the email. The room swirled around her. She was drunk.

'You have a cat?' Janine looked at her, shocked. 'You do not seem like the type of person who'd have a cat. My fiancé thinks only psychos have cats,' she said seriously, and then cackled, clapping her hands together in front of her face as she laughed. The giant diamond on Janine's finger sparkled like a cartoon tooth.

'I'm full of surprises,' Claire said, bone-dry.

'Everyone's surprised you came out tonight,' Janine slurred.

'No one more than me,' Claire said as she started surveying the exits. She needed to go. She needed air. She felt itchy, wrapped suddenly in grief's scratchy blanket, its tight weave. 'Which is my cue to leave.'

'But we were just getting to know each other,' Janine said with a schoolgirl whine. 'I want to know all your secrets! All the goss!'

Claire gathered her bag in one hand, her phone in the other. She moved her body towards Janine's so she'd get the hint and get up, get out of her way.

Claire was worried that if Janine pressed, if Janine kept asking, she'd crack, she'd say something she regretted, she'd open up about Al and about Sydney, and if she said it out loud, it would become real. It would be impossible to ignore. And she certainly didn't trust Janine to keep anything to herself. She knew the way associates gossiped. Constantly searching for any crumb of information that could give them an inch of power, a way in, a leg up.

They'd invited her to the pub in the past and she'd always said no. She'd always found people's work camaraderie strange. Grown adults with their work husbands and work wives. Didn't they have real friends outside the office? Didn't they have other people they'd rather spend their Friday nights with? Claire could've gone to Al's family dinner. She could've texted Ev. She could've called Annie and Nathan. She could've invited herself over to her cousin Nikola's. She was always welcome there. Or she used to be. They'd not seen each other in . . . she tried to count, but the last time was too long ago for her to hang a date on. She looked at her colleagues and wondered if maybe she was the sad one. The uptight one who kept her cards too close to her chest. She'd seen the way they looked at each other when she'd agreed to go out: raised eyebrows, sideways glances, a few approving nods, one surprised shrug. Now that she was drunk, Claire regretted coming to the pub. She regretted staying this late. She regretted having this job, this life. She wanted to start over. She could start over. The idea of Sydney shimmered on the horizon like a mirage.

They'd left the office at nine, Claire already tipsy after two champagnes. They'd scored a coveted corner spot at one of the fancy city pubs full of other city people trying to blow off steam. She bought a bottle of champagne for the table, some hot chips that went cold, remained largely untouched. She picked at them anyway. Then there were gin and tonics, there were conversations about work that bored her. She noticed people going to the bathrooms in twos, threes. No one invited her to go with them and she was glad.

She looked at her phone again, at the fluffy pastures of Crunchie's tummy, and she pined for her. For the reliability of her affection, for her constant attention.

'See you Monday,' Claire said to Janine as she stood.

The room wobbled as if being viewed through water. Claire imagined the alcohol filling her body all the way up to her eye line.

She pushed through the pub's doors, desperate for air, and walked straight into the broad chest of a man.

'Well, look who it is,' he said in a surprisingly shrill voice for his size. She didn't need to look up to know who it was but she looked anyway. His jawless face, that big fat nose, those pencil-thin lips. Ev was right. He did look like Shrek.

'Hi, Ed,' she said.

'You're the last person I'd expect to see out having fun with the plebs,' he said.

'Special occasion,' Claire said coldly.

'My fiancée's in there,' he said. 'She works with you – Janine.'

Claire thought of the big ring on Janine's long finger.

'She doesn't know about us, of course. I don't want to make it weird.'

'Congratulations,' Claire said. 'Janine is lovely.'

'She talks about you. Says you're still too good to hang out with the rest of them, that you still don't give anything away.' His voice was bitter.

'That's . . . nice,' Claire said. She felt panicked, desperate to get away from him, desperate to go somewhere. To be anywhere but here. She wanted to yell at him.

'I reckon I dodged a bullet there,' he said, still blocking the footpath so Claire couldn't get around him.

His anger with her was not without reason. The way she cut and ran. She remembered how she'd felt when she found the ring in his bedside table. It was so gaudy. The giant teardrop diamond, the ring of smaller diamonds around it. It was the most un-Claire thing Claire had ever seen. She knew then that Ed had never known her and would never really know her. And she realised that if she didn't leave him then, she would start to lose herself too. It was as if a starting pistol had gone off in her head. She put the ring back where she found it and twenty minutes later, when he arrived home with the Indian takeaway he'd gone to collect, she told him she was done. That it was over.

She took her stuff that night and hadn't seen Ed in the seven years since, despite his desperate attempts to win her back. Despite the bouquets of flowers he sent to the office, despite the six months of sporadic late night phone calls, the voicemail messages that consisted either of him begging her to come back or telling her what a bitch she was. Sometimes both in one night. Eventually, she let Al answer the phone and tell Ed where to go. It worked.

'I'd like to go now,' she said. 'Please move.' And she pushed past him then broke into a light jog as she crossed the road, despite there being no oncoming traffic to avoid.

'Go on, run away – you're good at that,' he yelled after her, and it took all her strength not to turn back and thump her fists into his chest, to scream all her pain into his face. But she just kept moving. The forward motion felt good.

She hadn't drunk this much in a while. She'd been too busy at work. She'd been going in on weekends, staying late, sometimes working all night. The last time she'd had too much to drink, the last time she and Al did anything properly social together, was a party at the Nobles' in April.

•

SHE KNEW AL hated these things. The soirees. She knew he hated that the firm called them soirees. She only ever called them that as a joke to Al, though she and Al didn't joke that much anymore.

She always briefed him on the way there: whose house it was, how important they were, which of his best stories not to tell (most of them), which topics to avoid and with whom. And even though he hated them, she'd never had to worry about Al at these parties before. They were important to her so they became important to him. Not like Ed. Claire would feel nervous just leaving Ed alone with her friends. Often for good reason. She could remember multiple occasions when she'd come back from the bathroom to find him in an argument with Ev about how you can't say anything anymore, about political correctness gone mad. Ev had sighed with relief when she finally left him.

This party, however, was the first since November. It was in her honour: a guestlist of all the partners, the board. A celebration of her promotion. This time, she was nervous.

It was only ever the managing partners who hosted – allegedly a tradition from back when they started the firm and took turns eating at each other's homes every week. Their houses were all impressive, enormous, extravagant, a block back from the sea, or in leafy streets with tall gates, big walls, expansive gardens.

They'd decided to get the train there and Uber back – a fiscal decision both of them regretted, especially after leaving the house without umbrellas. By the time they arrived, frazzled and out of breath from the walk from the train station, they were soggy from the rain. They stood for a second at the front gate. This was one of the leafy-street houses. Vine-covered walls, the leaves turning red with the autumn weather. The street was slightly elevated, so the sparkling tops of the city's buildings were just visible.

Al looked up at the house silently; he seemed to stop breathing altogether, and it wasn't until she linked one arm through his and led him up the driveway (if she didn't, she wasn't sure he'd come) that she heard him start again. This was a thing she'd noticed him doing lately. Since. Holding his breath for a long time. Sometimes in bed she would panic for a second but then she'd see his chest rise as the air was expelled from his lungs in one long sigh.

At the top of the glistening driveway, the front door was open. There was the din of voices down the long hall. Claire unbuttoned her coat, hung it up away from the others so she wouldn't get them wet. She waited while Al stood stock-still at the end of a long Persian hall runner, his damp coat still on. She knew what he was thinking: if he kept his coat on, they wouldn't have to stay long. By keeping his coat on he was mounting a silent protest about being there at all. She knew what he really wanted to do was Uber home and watch an episode of one of the four shows they promised to only watch together so never got around to watching. Claire walked up to him, unzipped the coat seductively, practically dragged it off him.

'Please just try to pretend like you're happy for me,' she whispered as they made their way towards the voices, towards the warm light, towards the smell of delicious food, towards the small talk, the work-related banter, the torture.

At the end of the hallway, they were met with a loud cheer.

'The guest of honour,' Marnie Noble said, grabbing Claire by the shoulders and kissing her once on each cheek. 'Al, so nice to see you again.' She reached up and kissed him too. 'I forgot how handsome he is,' Marnie whispered loudly, and Claire laughed, Al blushed.

'Let me get you a drink.' Marnie clapped her hands together enthusiastically. She was the perfect host: warm, exuberant, generous. She was beautiful too, Claire thought. She always forgot that about Marnie, and then she'd see her in person and remember she had that sexy late-forties, TV star thing about her. A Connie Britton-ness.

'I'll go,' Al said. 'Just tell me where. Champagne?' he asked Claire, and, before she had time to answer, he disappeared in the direction Marnie had vaguely indicated.

Claire made her way slowly around the room, greeting everyone. She noticed the high ceilings, shelves and shelves of books; those that couldn't fit upright were jammed in on their sides. In between some of the books were little statues, African masks collected while on safari, wooden carvings of Polynesian women. She hoped Al wouldn't see them but she knew he'd go looking, make a point of his disapproval.

Most of the questions Claire was asked first were about Al: 'Where did he go?' 'How does a man that tall disappear?' 'What does he do again?' And: 'Where is he from?'

Fifteen minutes and a lot of small talk later, Al still hadn't reappeared with her drink. She excused herself from a profoundly boring conversation about kitchen remodelling, located the kitchen (it looked recently remodelled), and found Al talking to John Noble. Her shoulders tightened. He was number one on the list of people she wanted to impress.

'Oh, Claire, there you are. I was just telling your better half all of my best jokes. Oh, oh.' John Noble wiggled his fingers excitedly. 'You'll like this one, Al.'

Claire hadn't known it was possible for her whole body to cringe, but it did. She braced herself.

'Okay, why are camels called –'

'Oh god, John,' Marnie interrupted from the door. 'Please don't torture these poor people with your jokes.' Marnie stood beside him, put a hand on the back of his neck. A code developed over decades together that Claire intuited meant, *Stop talking now.*

Al excused himself and left the kitchen without looking at her, a glass of champagne in each hand. Claire was sure one was meant for her, but she poured herself another just in case Al drank both. She wouldn't have blamed him.

With her glass full, Claire turned to talk to John Noble, but he was busy making himself a plate of food.

Returning to the living room, she tried to position herself between Al and anyone who might ask him something stupid. Still, the questions came. 'So where is your family from?' (Box Hill.) 'Where were you born?' (The Epworth.) 'Have you spent much time in the Middle East? (Two weeks when he was fifteen.) She was sure the answers disappointed them, wouldn't quench their thirst.

She stood next to Al for as long as she could, an energy moat, a protector, but then she was summoned to the other side of the room for a conversation about the Native Title Act of 1993 and lost him again.

'How old were you when it was introduced?' John Noble asked, his arm settling around her shoulders.

'Nine,' Claire said with mock sheepishness.

She didn't see Al slip out, but she was sure he was pretending to look for the bathroom. He'd got good at disappearing.

Forty-five minutes later, she excused herself from one of John Noble's stories and went in search of Al again.

She walked through a formal dining room, down a long hall. At the end of it was a study: big desk, big chair, more books, a sculpted bust of a woman. Claire ran a hand over the stone.

She saw movement from the corner of her eye, gasped at the shock of it. But it was just her reflection in the darkened window. She looked like she was staring into a funhouse mirror – her head oblong, face wonky.

She found Al, finally, sitting on the back deck watching the rain make tiny ripples across the surface of the pool. He was drinking a can of beer, and there were three empty cans on the ground around him. He seemed peaceful in the quiet.

'There you are,' Claire said, shivering in the damp night air. 'Sorry if that got intense in there. All those questions.' She grimaced for effect but he didn't see her.

'It's fine,' he said. 'I love answering questions about Islamic fundamentalism at a party.'

'No, they didn't?' Claire said, she put a hand on each cheek to show her disgust. Munch's *The Scream*, that little blue-and-yellow emoji. 'I'm so sorry.' She walked up close to him and eased her whole body between his open legs. He didn't put his hands on her, didn't wrap himself around her like he would've done before. Before.

'If it's any consolation, I was getting harangued about something I said in a mediation a year and a half ago,' she said.

'Not really,' Al said. 'What do you say we do an Irish goodbye?'

'I always thought an Irish goodbye was one where you spend an hour saying goodbye to everyone? Because you're drunk, I guess.'

'That's racist,' Al said.

'Shut up.' She laughed. 'We have to do it properly.'

'Tell them I have to get up at five to pray,' Al said sarcastically.

Claire glared at him playfully.

'Let's go inside and start the process of leaving,' she said. 'As much as I love the idea of sneaking off, they did this for me. I have to do the classy thing.'

Al groaned.

'They did all this to show off. It's not the same.'

'We at least have to say thank you. Tell them how nice their house is again. Play the game for five more minutes and then we can go.'

'Okay,' he said, and he followed her back inside.

THEY WERE ALMOST out of there. They'd kissed a dozen wine-warmed cheeks, shaken hands, said thank you thank you thank you, each received a long hug from Marnie then, uncharacteristically, one from John. They were halfway down the hall when they saw Patti, the executive assistant, coming towards them from the front door. She reeked of cigarette smoke, wobbled slightly on her too-high heels. She had to be almost sixty. Her leather trousers were too loose on her bird-thin legs; her tiny arms poked out of a billowing white sleeveless top.

Patti seemed like she would've been a whole lot of fun once upon a time. A free spirit. But now, everything about her felt put on, from her dry, dyed hair to the softness of her voice. She was always talking about everything with all of her feelings; every sad story she heard was the saddest story anyone had ever told, every joke she heard the funniest. She was a people pleaser, spineless. And there was no way out except to go past her.

'Darlings, before you go,' Patti said, 'I've been meaning to ask. Those friends of yours, who lost their son. So sad, so tragic. My goodness.' She clutched her hand to her heart as though she was going into cardiac arrest.

'It is very sad,' Al said, his voice higher and tighter than Claire had ever heard it. She was sure Patti meant well; after all, Patti couldn't know that just by bringing it up, she was sticking a finger into an open wound whose bleeding was barely staunched.

'What were their names again?' Patti asked, her face grimacing with pain that didn't belong to her. Claire sensed Al fidgeting beside her.

'Nathan and Annie,' Claire said.

'How are they doing?'

'They're okay,' Claire said. 'Getting there.' It was not the truth. The truth was that Annie was a shell of herself, no longer sweet and kind – no longer anything, really. Claire couldn't tell

Patti that all Nathan did was work now, that the two of them were slowly drifting apart. She'd read somewhere – because that's what she did in the early days: read and read and read about grief, visiting forums where bereaved parents shared stories of children lost – that the reason so many couples broke up after losing a child was because their grief didn't sync. One would be in the denial stage, another anger. She worried that there wouldn't be a Nathan-and-Annie for much longer. She worried about her and Al, too. But every time she started to think about it, about how much had changed since it happened, she felt as if she were being constricted, crushed from the inside out, a reverse garbage compactor. So it was easier not to think about it, to just knuckle down, to carry on. If she ignored it, it couldn't be real.

'How was it that he died again?' Patti asked. 'It was an accident, wasn't it?'

Claire heard Al sigh.

'He choked,' Claire said with a quiet matter-of-factness. 'On a marshmallow.'

Patti gasped. 'Oh yes, yes.' She let tears come to her eyes but not fall. 'Those poor things. That poor baby. I will keep them in my thoughts,' she added, her mouth so downturned she looked like a hammerhead shark.

'Thank you,' Claire said. 'I'm sure they'd appreciate that. I think our Uber is here, though, so we should go.'

'Of course,' Patti said, her eyes already dry, as if a switch had been flicked. Claire didn't trust her. 'Take care and see you

Monday, darling.' And she was gone, wafting off to another part of the house like stale air.

Claire watched Al stride down the drive. She knew what was coming. His anger was like a tornado: fast and destructive.

'How dare she!' he yelled when they got to the bottom of the driveway. 'How fucking dare she!'

Claire stayed back a few paces. Maybe if he got it all out now, out here, they could have a quiet ride home.

'What makes people think it's any of their goddamn business?'

The Uber pulled up in front of them and Al climbed into the back, behind the passenger seat. Claire waited for him to budge over, but he closed the door and put his seatbelt on. Here we go, she thought. She walked around behind the car and climbed in next to him.

'Hello, how are you?' she said to the driver, hoping he'd chat and diffuse the tension.

But the driver wasn't going to play along. 'Ali?' he asked, and when Al confirmed with a noise he set off, the car's tyres swishing on the wet road.

'John Noble was flirting with you,' Al said, not looking at her, instead looking out the window as the leafy streets turned into two-lane roads.

They stopped and started behind a tram.

'He was flirting with you too,' Claire said. 'He flirts.' She reached for his hand, his leg, anything to show that she was still his, but he pulled away. 'It's what he does.' She reached even further and got him this time. Got his thigh in her hand and squeezed it.

'The difference is' – he picked her hand up and put it down on the seat – 'I don't flirt back.'

'Oh, come on.' She put her hand in her lap. 'I laughed at his joke, I hugged him goodbye. It's not the same thing.'

'*Oh, John, you're terrible*,' Al said in what she presumed was meant to be her voice, made extra whiny, extra flirty.

Claire winced, hurt. She'd not seen him jealous before. It was ugly on him.

'He is terrible,' Claire said with an exasperated sigh. 'His jokes are terrible. But he's my boss. He's the one who decides if I have a job. Being nice to him means we can buy a house soon.'

They were silent for a full minute. She saw Al catch the eye of their Uber driver, who looked at him in the rear-view mirror – out of sympathy maybe. Or perhaps as a way to tell him he was overreacting, that he was being the idiot. He *was* overreacting. She didn't flirt with John. She respected him but that was as far as it went.

'That's not what this is about, anyway,' Claire said, looking straight ahead.

'What *what* is about?'

'This mood. These moods you've been having.'

'Okay, what's it about then? Please enlighten all of us. Are you ready for this, Yash?'

The Uber driver held up a hand to say, *Leave me out of this.*

'It's about Nathan and Annie. It's your grief.'

They were quiet for another minute.

'Why did you lie to old what's-her-chops about how they're doing?' Al asked.

'Because I don't think either of them would appreciate me telling Patti fucking Saunders that they're not coping at all,' Claire said. 'That Ev's not coping, that we're not coping.' Al didn't say anything. Claire kept going. 'Grief is a rollercoaster ride, Al. And it's cumulative. These feelings . . . they can bring up stuff about others you've lost.'

She heard Al sigh.

'Like your mum, for example,' Claire added carefully.

'Don't bring her into this.'

'Okay,' Claire said. She looked out the window at the raindrops shining like tiny stars caught by passing lights.

The driver slowed down, pulled up next to a row of parked cars. Al got out before they'd come to a complete stop, slammed the door, stormed up the two front steps.

'Thank you, and sorry,' she said to Yash as she stepped out into the wet street and watched Al fish fruitlessly in each pocket for his keys. Claire walked slowly, sadly, up the steps behind him. On the other side of the door, Crunchie's hungry meows were audible, frantic.

'I'm sorry,' Al said tenderly as she turned the key in the lock.

'It's going to take time,' she said. 'But we'll get there.'

She opened the door and a ball of fluff ran rings around their legs.

'Who wants some dinner?' Al asked in the slightly higher voice he affected only when talking to the cat.

Claire watched the two of them scamper down the hall together. She wasn't sure she knew where 'there' was, let alone how they'd find their way.

•

WITHOUT THINKING, CLAIRE had found herself back at her desk. She had a McDonald's meal deal spread out in front of her: Big Mac, fries, a drink. At the self-serve screen, she'd added six nuggets too. It was two thirty am. She opened her laptop and while the screen came to life she dunked a nugget into the little tub of barbecue sauce. Her stomach rumbled as she shoved the whole thing into her mouth. Password in, email open. Another nugget dunked in the sickly sweet goo to rally her courage. She read Helen's email in full.

> Team's on board. Just got to run it up the ladder.
> A bit of box ticking to do but the job's as good as yours.
> Glad I finally got you ;)
> H

She read the email, picked up a handful of fries, toasted herself with them, shovelled them in.

'You did it,' she said aloud. She slapped her laptop shut again and looked around the office at the things she'd take with her. The stapler she'd bought and written her name on. A box of tea. The gym gear stashed in her bottom drawer. Her notice period was three months but they'd probably put her on gardening leave. It'd give her enough time to find a place, to get Crunchie settled. She thought of Al. Maybe a move would be good for him too? Both of them, a fresh start. A new chance to get back in sync.

She thought of telling him about the job. How would he feel when he found out that she'd gone through this without him? That she hadn't considered his feelings, his wants, his future? Their future? But she had, hadn't she? Hadn't she spent the whole of the last year worrying about him?

She thought again of the couples she'd read about, their grief misaligned, out of sync. Cracks appearing. She and Al weren't just orbiting at different speeds, they seemed to be in separate solar systems. She felt jealous of Ev. To be going through this unencumbered by the weight of someone else's grief. How she was able to float down this river at her own pace. Ev, who was never afraid to admit she was wrong. Ev, who changed the course of her life just like that. Ev, who showed up for those kids at her school, who showed up for all of them every single day. Who refused to hide. There was no one like her.

She unwrapped the Big Mac, took a big bite, let the special sauce drip down her chin. She wished her colleagues could see her now. Wished Ed could see her now. She thought about what he'd said. He was right: the instinct ran through her like blood.

She thought about her grandfather, her grandmother. Their skin rough like leather from European summers spent without knowledge of an ozone layer and UV levels, without zinc across noses and sand stuck to sunscreen-covered legs. Even in their coffins, the two of them dying within a year of each other, their skin escaped the pallor of death. She remembered their faces, eyes closed, peaceful. Her last encounter with death was so violent in comparison. Blue-lipped and surrounded by panic. One year ago. She raised a handful of fries again. 'Happy birthday, little one,' she said. Maybe somewhere he could hear her. Maybe somewhere he knew she was thinking of him, missing him.

She finished her Big Mac, scrunched up the wrapper and shoved it inside the nugget box. She chucked them both into her office bin with the last of the fries, and the large Sprite she'd ordered, the sweetness of which made her throat hurt. Her hunger satiated, she sat back in her chair.

She felt tired. So tired. So sick of being so tired. Her head hurt. An ache that stretched across her forehead like a damp cloth placed there as if to calm a fever. She riffled through the second drawer of her desk and found some ibuprofen. She took her discarded drink from the bin, swallowed two sugar-coated pills with two sips of Sprite, then chucked it back in. She wondered if her body would ever feel right. If she would ever feel good again. Or if she'd carry this around with her forever, this feeling wrapped around her like a vine.

Perhaps if she just slept for an hour, two, just rested her head while the painkillers kicked in. She kicked off her shoes and curled up on the sofa along the side wall of her office, her good linen suit jacket a blanket over her aching body. Just an hour, she thought. Just a rest. The room spun a little at first, but soon she felt herself drifting through darkness as if falling from a great height, just her and the stars, her and the bats and the night sky.

Twenty

EV WOKE WITH HER FACE spit-slicked, drool darkening the fabric of her pillowcase. She felt sweaty between her boobs, used her pyjamas to wipe herself down. It was Saturday. It was November third.

She was proud she'd gone to bed at all. She'd jolted awake on the couch at one am, all the lights blazing, laptop screen black, battery dead. It would've been easy to reach for the light, go back to sleep, but she rallied herself, closed her laptop, turned the lights off, got out of her clothes and into some pyjamas, and slept. On her bedside table, the night-time cold and flu tablet pack. She'd decided between sofa and bed, that she needed some help. She was glad for it.

Ev lay still on her back, worried that if she moved a thudding headache would arrive, bringing with it curdled guts. The last thing she needed today was a hangover. From the corner of her eye she could see a white feather from her pillow tangled in a curl of her hair. She left it there. Her neighbours were up. She heard them through the walls: their low chatter, no words discernible. A young couple making Saturday morning breakfast together, moving around each other in the small kitchen.

She'd gone to sleep thinking of whales and now, as she lay, she searched her mind for peaceful thoughts, for memories of calm places. Not only was she slowly replacing the negative voices in her head, but the pictures too. Instead of the sight of his body, instead of the panicked screams, she would play back scenes from before. Strangely, it was never the big, significant memories that calmed her. Not her first day of law school, nor her first day teaching, not highlights from her first overseas trip (a week in Tokyo, thanks to those cheap Jetstar fares: big bowls of ramen ordered via machine, beers in the hidden bars of Piss Alley, standing in the middle of Shibuya while other tourists crisscrossed around her), but ordinary days back when things were just normal hard. Easy hard. She thought of the beach house, a weekend spent there a few years ago.

•

IT WAS FEBRUARY but the sky was grey, the sea mostly flat except for the white-crested peaks of little waves taking turns to lick the shore. Seagulls swooped and hollered, rallied in formation, headed inland. Ev had learned somewhere that seagulls head for dry land when there's a storm coming.

The beach was a thick white wedge that curved gently towards the headland a few kilometres away. A misty haze of sand and water and distance made the beach look foggy. She liked the way nature played tricks on you. Mirages on long roads. The way gravity made it feel like we weren't constantly moving.

She'd checked the weather apps in the lead-up to the weekend and neither had warned of rain. She trusted the birds more than she trusted the technology, though. Birds had no reason to lie, she thought, and shivered in the cool morning grey, shivered at the thought of the water, at the thinness of the air, at the sunlight that was trying to burst through the clouds but couldn't, wouldn't.

'I'm here,' Claire called as she jogged down the sand. 'I'm here.' When she reached Ev, she kissed her on the cheek and hugged her sideways. 'Happy birthday!'

'I thought I was going to have to go in on my own,' Ev said as Claire pulled away and looked out at the sea.

'Never!' Claire had a towel draped over her shoulder, her hair hidden by a hood. 'But are you sure you want to do this?'

'It's my only birthday wish,' Ev said.

'No Nath?' Claire asked.

'Still in bed,' Ev said and grimaced. Claire too.

'I wish they hadn't told us they're trying.' Claire screwed up her face. 'I just picture them having sex all the time. All that skin on skin.'

'I believe the kids call it raw-dogging,' Ev said, smiling. She'd overheard a student saying it and had to google it.

'No – please, no.' Claire covered her ears, clamped her eyes shut.

'Hey, at least they're still doing it, almost twenty years in,' Ev said, and Claire took her hands off her ears, thought about it for a second.

'I guess,' she said, shaking her head as if to dislodge the image.

It was heartening to see that it was possible, that two people could still be so in love after so long. Ev would never have believed it if she couldn't see it with her own eyes. Her dad took off the minute he found out her mum was pregnant. Her brother's dad stuck around a year and would pop back up every so often, waiting outside their flat with a cigarette in the corner of his mouth. Other boyfriends were there for a month and then gone, never to be spoken of again.

Nathan and Annie had made the announcement that they were trying for a baby at the dinner table the previous evening. No one was surprised, everyone was happy for them. They were. They toasted, clinked glasses across the table, both Annie and Nathan drinking soda water because of something they had read online about the correlation between drinking and low sperm count. Everyone else celebrated, overdid it.

While Ev was happy for them, she worried about what a baby would mean, what it would change and how. When her friends partnered, when they had kids, it meant she would drop further down the ladder of priorities. Sometimes she worried that no one gave her a second thought, no one worried about her.

They were at Nathan's parents' beach house (two storeys, five bedrooms, huge windows, wooden floors, pot-belly stove, a games room, big fat deck; across the road from the beach at Fairhaven, it was the kind of house people in cars slowed down to gawk at). They had gathered there for the weekend to celebrate Ev's birthday, a tradition that had started a decade earlier. Another tradition was the seven am birthday swim she insisted on. But that morning, Nathan was staying in bed. The world turned a little.

'Have you and Al' – Ev paused, not sure if she should proceed, if she wanted to know the answer – 'had any more conversations about it?'

Claire pushed her hood down; her hair blew wildly in the building wind.

'Only as an abstract thing that might happen at some point in the future,' Claire said, gesturing to the horizon as she talked, as if therein lay the answers. 'Although he said he'd stay home so I can go back to work straight away.'

'He's the last good man,' Ev said. She said this often as a joke, but deep down, she wondered if Claire really had met the last one. Her most recent interactions on Tinder, on Hinge, on Bumble all indicated she had.

'What about you?' Claire asked.

'Oh god,' Ev said. 'Surprise, surprise, I don't know what I want.' She pushed the hair out of her eyes. 'I always imagined I'd have more clarity about this stuff as I got older, but it only gets more complicated.' Claire nodded in agreement. 'All I know is that I can't do it on my own. Not after watching Mum struggle for all those years.'

'You've got time,' Claire said, and Ev wanted to believe she was right. She was thirty-three. She had plenty of time. 'You could freeze your eggs and worry about it later?'

'I can't really afford it,' Ev said. She'd spent hours googling it and discovered because she was doing it for 'social reasons' she didn't qualify for Medicare. It'd be at least three thousand dollars for the hormone injections alone. She'd thought about jabbing the needle through her skin at home and the image made her so sad she shut her laptop. She hated that she had to choose between a house deposit, a holiday, a family. Some women would never have it all. Some women just had to do without. 'I'm just going to stop thinking about it.'

'Denial is an excellent option,' Claire confirmed. 'Bloody hell, it should not be this cold in February.' She jumped up and down on the spot like a boxer right before the bell dings.

'Climate change, baby,' Ev said. 'We've got to make the most of this house before it gets swept away by the rising seas.'

Claire sighed in resignation.

'Shall we do this?' Ev gestured towards the water.

'Let's go.' Claire dropped her towel on the sand and kicked off her shoes. The two of them undressed silently beside each other, Ev pulling her jumper over her head, her t-shirt, leaving her track pants until last. They stood in their bathers, hugging themselves for warmth, then headed towards the water.

A wave rushed in and swamped their feet, their ankles.

'Jesus!' Claire shrieked. 'It's arctic.'

'It'll fix these hangovers – come on!' Ev called back to her as she started jogging into the waves.

The water felt like tiny knives cutting through the nerves that let her feel her feet, her legs. Waist deep, she dived under and surfaced quickly. The cold ripped the breath out of her lungs. She smoothed her hair back, wrung it out. She felt awake, alive, freezing cold. Claire was beside her, yelling profanities, and then she was under. They turned and ran back out together. The wind had rain in it now. The seagulls were right.

Ev reached the towels first and wrapped hers around her goosebumped, shaking body, leaned down for Claire's and passed it to her. Claire thanked her through chattering teeth. Ev towelled her mess of curly hair, wiped the water from her shoulders, her arms, held the towel against her bathers, hoping to suck some of the cold water away from her body. She started picking at her clothes that sat in a pile like a colourful ant hill. She looked up, saw a figure coming towards them. Even from a distance it was recognisable as Al. He was walking carefully, carrying something. Ev put her jumper on, pulled her bathers down underneath it, put her arms through. The dryness of it warmed her aching skin. Head out the top, she saw Al was carrying two mugs. One for him, one for Claire, she assumed. He kissed Claire on the cheek when he reached them, passed her a steaming hot cup of coffee.

'You're so lucky,' Ev said to them wistfully. 'No one would ever do that for me.'

'I'm doing it for you right now, you dickhead,' Al said and passed her the other mug: weak and white, just how she liked it. 'Happy birthday.'

'Oh.' She accepted it, embarrassed but grateful. 'Thank you.'

'Nice in then?' he asked as he pulled Claire in towards him to warm her shivering body.

Claire nestled in against him and he opened out the other arm and motioned for Ev to come in too. The three of them stood together for a few minutes absorbing all of Al's warmth, all of his love. It was going to be a good birthday, Ev thought. The cold water had cleared her head and she felt alive, she felt happy. It was going to be a good year; she felt it in her bones. Bones wouldn't lie either. What would be in it for them?

•

EV REACHED FOR her phone, charging under her pillow where she'd shoved it when she finally crawled into bed. She held it above her head and opened her messages, read back through the exchange she'd had with Emily the night before. They'd made a plan to see each other again on Tuesday night: dinner and a movie. Two dates in four days was a good sign, but Ev tried not to get ahead of herself. It felt so good to be excited, though, to feel something resembling hope. For her stomach to feel the flutter of butterflies instead of the churn of anxiety.

It was only eight. She wondered what Claire and Al were doing. If they'd had coffee and gone back to bed, Crunchie sandwiched between them while they did the Saturday quiz. She thought about Nathan and Annie waking up to another day without him. He'd already been gone half the time he'd been here. It was too quick. She missed him. God, she missed him. She had been worried that he'd change things between them for the worse but didn't consider all the joy he'd bring, how he'd change them all for the better. She remembered holding him at the hospital. Looking at that tiny person that was somehow half Annie and half Nathan but also a person all on his own. A tiny person that was all of her love for them combined, all of her love for them blossoming anew. It was too cruel that he was gone. She let the tears fall down her temples and soak into the pillows. She would let herself do this now, get it out, and then she'd go.

She wiped her eyes, her face. She readied herself and sat up. No headache, her guts were fine – her stomach rumbled almost violently – fine enough. She'd get up, shower, get dressed, ride down to Fitzroy North. She'd show up, just as she'd always done.

Twenty-one

NATHAN WOKE BEFORE ANNIE AND lay looking at the pure white light across the ceiling, the sun from the bright spring morning, from the clear blue sky.

It took a few seconds after he woke, as it did most mornings. He loved those few seconds of nothingness. But then he'd remember.

His mouth would go dry. He'd feel fatigued right into the marrow of his bones. His eyes heavy, jaw clicking from the nighttime grinding of his teeth. Some mornings, he had the feeling like a hand was pressing on the back of his head, a feeling like someone was brushing the inside of his rib cage with the vigour of an old-timey shoeshine. Sometimes he'd experience just one of these feelings, sometimes all of them at once. His grief was a lucky dip. He wondered, and this was the real kicker, how, when it felt so terrible, so constant and so present, so unrelenting, it could also be so boring. He would wake up, he would remember, he would be pummelled by his grief and think: not this again; not this, still.

Annie stirred next to him, rolled over. He sensed she was awake but she kept her eyes closed.

The previous evening swam into his mind. His mother, his sister, Ruby, the look of terror in Al's eyes when he saw Nathan walking towards him. He'd seen it before. People were scared of what he and Annie represented: the truth of how quickly things can change, how easily everything can be taken away. That no one was safe. That there were no guarantees. We wear that with us, he thought, carrying it from room to room, house to house, carrying it into the dairy aisle of the supermarket.

Annie's eyes opened, blinked a few times as she focused on him.

'Where were you last night?' she croaked, stretching her arms above her like a sleepy cat, like a caricature of someone who had just woken up.

'Toorak,' he said, too tired to explain everything that had happened.

'Cherie called,' Annie said. She pulled herself up, shuffled her back against the headboard, made a pillow into a backrest as if she was readying herself to stay there for a while. She used to do this whenever she wanted to talk. Back when she used to want to talk.

'Of course she did,' Nathan said, and he rolled over on his side, propped his head up with his hand.

'She said you yelled at her.'

Annie picked at some sleep in her eye, removing it with her fingernail. Nathan noticed empty pill packaging on her bedside table. The last of the sleeping pills punched from its hole the night before. She hadn't stirred when he'd come to bed, when he'd eased one foot from his shoe, steadying himself with the toe of the other. Not when he'd accidentally let them fall on the hardwood floor of the wardrobe. She hadn't woken when he'd turned the bathroom light on, brushed his teeth, examined his tired eyes in the mirror, done a runny shit, the rot inside him bursting its way out.

'She said you were disrespectful and she deserves an apology.'

'Yeah,' he said with an empty laugh. 'She probably does.'

'What did you say to her?' Annie asked.

'I told her to go fuck herself,' Nathan said, and Annie looked at him deadpan, disappointed, but she didn't say anything, didn't ask any more questions. It was as if she knew it had been coming. Nathan wasn't so sure of that this morning. In the cold light of day, he felt embarrassed, guilty. He'd apologise, make amends.

'I thought you'd come home straight after,' Annie said.

'I went to Fran's,' Nathan said. 'I needed to talk to someone who understands what she's like.'

'Oh.' Annie sounded hurt. 'I'd have liked to see them too.' She tucked her hair behind her ear.

'They said they'd come over on the weekend,' Nathan said. 'But look – Ruby made us a present.'

Nathan reached over to the bedside table for the book, that precious thing. Annie adjusted herself, sat further up, straightened the sheet over her lap. He could see the outline of her body under her pyjamas.

He put the book in her hands. She looked down at the cover. At his name painted in colourful letters. She traced each letter with her index finger.

'Oh, Ruby,' she said. She looked at the cover quietly. 'I always liked how their names ended with the same letters,' she said as tears ran down her cheeks. They seemed to appear with no effort required from her body. As if crying was as natural to her body now as breathing.

'Me too.' He leaned closer but didn't touch her.

She opened the book and read every caption, studied every photo. At the third page, she stopped to let out a loud sob. He passed her a tissue from the box that they'd taken to keeping on the bedside table a year ago. A box each. She blew her nose, passed the tissue back to him, and he swapped it for another.

'She's so lovely,' Annie said and shook her head. A tear dropped onto one of the pages: a photo of a drawing they'd done together, Ruby in charge of the outline. Nathan remembered her handing the crayons to him, instructing him where to colour.

'We've stopped saying his name,' Nathan said, and Annie looked up at him. 'Have you noticed? We hardly talk about him, and when we do, we never say his name.'

Annie's breath shuddered in and out. She tried to keep in another sob, but it was stronger than her.

'It just hurts too much,' she said.

'I know, but this hurts too,' he said. 'Acting as if he never existed, not talking about him or remembering – that hurts so much.' He was crying now.

'I don't know how to keep going,' Annie said, forgoing the tissue to wipe her face with the back of her hand. 'Being a mum was all I ever wanted. I was good at it.' She made a noise. Primal, animal-like. A gulp that was also a moan. 'I don't know how to be in the world without him. I don't remember what it was like before.'

'We were so lucky to have him, to have known him.'

Annie nodded through her tears. 'I know that people think I should be over it by now.'

'No one thinks that,' he said.

'Or they think I should be back at work or that we should have another baby. That we're doing it wrong.'

'They don't.'

'Your mum thinks that,' Annie said.

'Everyone just wishes this could be easier for you.'

Annie continued turning the pages, reading Ruby's words.

Nathan watched her. He loved watching her, loved the little lobes of her ears, her cheeks that blushed easily, her long eyelashes, the lines that appeared at the corners of her eyes when she laughed. He hadn't seen them in a while. She stopped reading and looked up.

'Do you ever worry that it's never going to get better? I'm scared there'll never be an hour when it doesn't hurt like this,' Annie said.

'Sometimes I feel like I can't see him in my head, I can't smell him or hear him anymore. He's slipping away.'

'I talk to him,' Annie said. 'Sometimes I talk to him like he's still here. It helps. God, I just miss him so much.' She reached out and put her hand on his; their fingers interlocked. 'I miss him.'

'I miss him too.'

He unlocked his fingers and put his arm around her shoulders. He pulled her towards him, kissed the top of her hair. She looked up at him and he kissed her on the lips too.

'Your breath smells like garbage,' Annie said and smiled. She kissed him again before rolling over and putting her slippers on. She lifted a patterned robe from where it had been draped over the chair in the corner. 'I'm going to make him –' She paused, steadied herself. 'Toby,' she said, her eyes closed. 'I'm going to make Toby a birthday breakfast.' She picked up Ruby's book and left the room.

He stood too. In the bathroom he turned the shower on, stepped out of his underpants and into the too-hot water, let it redden his skin, let himself be enveloped in the steamy, hot mess of it all.

Twenty-two

IT WAS FIFTEEN MINUTES DOWN the creek path to Fitzroy North, a little more with a stop-off. Ev hadn't noticed Claire when she chained her bike to the fence. It was only when she walked through the gate that she saw her. Asleep, it seemed, her head resting on her arms, which were resting on her knees. She was wearing her gym gear. The gate creaked closed behind her. Claire didn't move.

Ev looked around at the garden as she walked up the path. Annie's makeover/meltdown (I would watch that reality TV show, Ev thought) looked even worse the next day. Everything she'd pulled from the ground was either dying or already dead. Things that were green were yellowing, things that were yellowing were marching towards brown. The colours at the end of a bruise, the colours of death.

'Hello,' Ev said, and Claire groaned. She didn't look up when Ev spoke. She didn't look up when Ev sat down on the step beside her.

'Are you injured? Do I need to be worried?'

'Not physically,' Claire said, turning her head to face Ev, resting her cheek back on her arm. 'You're a sight for sore eyes.' She leaned her body closer to Ev's warmth.

'What happened to you?'

'I slept at the office.'

'But why do you smell like that?' Ev asked.

'I showered at the gym, I promise,' Claire took a whiff of herself. 'But I also threw up.'

Ev frowned, worried. 'Sad sick, sick sick, drinking sick or too-much-exercise sick?' she asked.

Claire rarely got sick. Claire hardly drank. Claire often exercised for too long. Ev had to catch her once when she fainted after a hot yoga class, buy her some Deep Heat once when she went for a jog and accidentally ran a half-marathon.

'Sad sick and drinking sick,' Claire said. 'My case settled and I decided I should celebrate with the team.'

Ev didn't say anything, just nodded at Claire to go on.

'I ran into Ed,' Claire said.

'And that's when you puked?' Ev asked. 'On him, I hope?'

'I wish. I drank too much and I ate McDonald's and I slept at the office and I went to the gym and I went on the treadmill and then I vomited.'

'Wow,' Ev said and squeezed her. 'And I thought Annie's was the loudest cry for help.'

'What did Annie do?' Claire sat up, looked at Ev. 'Is she okay?'

Ev motioned to the garden in front of them, couldn't believe Claire hadn't noticed when she came through the gate. That made Ev worry even more. And where was Al? He hadn't texted her looking for Claire. Had he known she wasn't coming home? She wondered if this was something that happened often.

'Shit,' Claire said. 'What a mess.'

'I thought you were doing okay,' Ev said. 'I should've checked, I'm sorry.'

'No, it's all right – I thought I was doing okay too,' Claire said.

'Sneaks up on you sometimes, huh?'

'Real stealthy.' Claire looked at Ev properly, as if her eyes had only just come into focus. 'What about you – do anything silly last night?'

'I watched four episodes of *Law and Order: SVU* and fell asleep marking history assignments,' Ev lied. She thought about Emily and her stomach flipped.

'Is four episodes a normal evening or a cry for help?' Claire asked.

'I think four is a hobby, five is a problem.' Ev smiled. She'd definitely watched five in a row before, churned through a twenty-two-episode season in a weekend unable to move from the couch. The sadness was paralysing at first.

'Good to know,' Claire said.

'I wonder what it's like in there.' Ev turned to look at the house that still seemed eerily quiet without Toby's screams, Toby's tears, his chatter, the loudness of his laugh. 'Shall we find out?' she asked, standing, extending a hand to help Claire up.

Claire took it, let Ev lift her onto her feet, but she overbalanced, used Ev's shoulders to right herself.

'I'm okay,' she said, and Ev could tell she was mostly rallying herself. 'I'm okay.'

Ev gripped Claire's forearms until she was steady.

'Should we have brought something?' Claire asked.

'We're here,' Ev said. 'That's enough.' And she rang the doorbell.

Nothing. The house felt still, empty. She waited. Then footsteps coming downstairs, Annie at the door in a robe.

'Oh good, it's you. I thought you were another bunch of flowers,' she said.

Ev hugged Annie on the way past. She felt all her friend's bones, felt all her sadness. She'd always been thin but now she felt barely there.

In the kitchen, Ev unpacked some things from her backpack that she'd picked up on the way, sliding them into the shelves of the fridge. She'd expected to see Nathan in the kitchen but it was just the three of them. She sat at the bench next to Claire while Annie made them coffee. Perfect flat whites from a professional-looking machine. Annie entertaining, just as she had a year ago.

Ev couldn't help but think about the difference between then and now. This picture, this thought, too powerful to replace; too immediate, too sad to divert.

•

SHE ARRIVED EARLY for the party. In a delicate balancing act she'd perfected in her role as a teacher (she was always carrying too much stuff: folders of the kids' work, the readings she had to scrub up on, a laptop, a bike helmet), she lifted her knee and balanced the box of lolly bags she'd brought on the flat of her thigh while she unlatched the gate, then scooped it up again as she ducked through an archway of colourful balloons. She liked that Annie had chosen a rainbow instead of blue. She hoped it was a dig at the politics of her in-laws, but she suspected it was purely at Toby's insistence. Over the past six months, he'd become obsessed with rainbows. Ev had taught him what ROYGBIV meant, taught him a song to go with it.

She let herself in, the front door unlocked.

'Helloooo,' she called down the hall. She was there to help despite not being asked, despite being told that everything was under control.

'Oh, thank god you're here,' Annie called from the kitchen.

'Lolly bags as promised,' Ev said, and placed the box down on the end of the bench where there was already an impressive spread laid out: perfectly cut carrots next to bowls of dip, cupcakes (vegan), cupcakes (gluten-free). Ev felt tired just looking at it all.

She'd spent the morning packing mostly sugar-free lollies into little party bags: dinosaurs and sour worms, marshmallows. All the bags tied up with ribbons Annie had supplied. Even that small task had exhausted her. If the last two years had taught her anything, it was that motherhood seemed tedious at times; often a repetition of thankless tasks. A lolly dinosaur in the bag, a worm, a dinosaur, a worm, a marshmallow, a dinosaur.

'Help me,' Annie begged. 'Please.'

She was wearing an apron, her hair straightened, her make-up perfectly done, her cheeks flushed. 'You look beautiful,' Ev said and kissed Annie on the cheek. Her hands were covered in mushed-up egg yolk. 'Are you making devilled eggs?' Ev asked and Annie nodded. She looked like she might cry.

'Toby loves them,' Annie said. Of course he did.

'Where's your husband?' Ev asked.

'On a call. Some crisis. It's important, apparently.'

Ev smiled at her sympathetically. She knew Nathan was considered a Very Important Man who dealt with other Very Important Men. He was always having urgent meetings about top-secret things. He was always ducking away for phone calls. Sometimes, if he couldn't find a private spot, he'd cover his mouth so no one could read his lips. He'd fly up to Canberra at least once a fortnight, leaving early in the morning, coming back late, or staying over in an okay hotel paid for by someone else. Annie told her once that she'd often find receipts in his jacket pocket when she'd take them to be dry-cleaned. A whisky at the hotel bar. Just one, then bed.

'Okay, put me to work,' Ev said and rolled up her sleeves, taking over the mashing of yolks from Annie while she rushed upstairs to get Toby dressed, to get Nathan off the phone. Ev piped the yolks back into the whites, sprinkled them with paprika; she made a pitcher of sugar-free ginger cordial; she filled the drinks tubs with ice – one with juice for the kids, the other with champagne for the adults. She walked to the edge of the living room where the big bi-fold doors were open and stood for a moment in the breeze. Annie had done it again: the backyard looked like one of those kid's birthday parties you saw in American movies, with trestle tables and chairs set up, balloons, seats for the grown-ups, a games area for the children. A year earlier, it'd been just as fancy, just as stressful, just as successful.

She heard a giggle from behind her and a pair of little arms grabbed at her legs.

'There he is,' she said. 'The birthday boy.' She turned and picked Toby up, a hand in each armpit. He was dressed in a little checked shirt, slacks, his curly brown hair like a mop atop his tiny head. His shirt lifted over his belly and she blew raspberries on it, one after the other. 'One for every day you've been alive,' she said and started counting. By ten he was giggling and squirming and she stopped, lifted him high above her head and then put him down onto the floor.

He ran back into the house screaming joyfully, and Ev saw that Annie's parents and sister (who had Annie's wavy blonde hair, Annie's warm, open face, her same long nose) had let themselves in. They had armfuls of presents, despite the invitation saying no presents. And if last year was anything to go by, they would be full of trucks and cars, a train set. Ev could see that the boxes were all wrapped in blue paper. She greeted them with a kiss on the cheek and left them to sit around, to start eating and drinking. She pulled a bottle of champagne from the tub of melting ice and took it inside, where she found Annie crying in loud, racking sobs in a corner of the kitchen.

'Oh no, what is it, what happened?' In front of her, Ev spotted a tray of homemade sausage rolls, some of them blackened, crisped to death across the top. She put the champagne down next to the tray and hugged her friend silently.

'I'm so tired,' Annie whispered.

'I know,' Ev whispered. 'You've done an amazing job. And even if this whole thing was catered by Nigella Lawson, it would still not be good enough for Cherie. She's always going to find something to pick on.'

'You're right.' Annie laughed through the tears. Ev let go of her. 'I just want it to be perfect. Not for her – for me and for Nathan, and for Toby.' Annie pointed at the mop of brown hair that was now tearing around the garden.

'He won't remember the sausage rolls. We'll just take a few photos and tell him it was perfect,' Ev said, smiling. 'Now, how about we celebrate what's really important.' She ripped the foil off the top of the bottle.

'His birthday,' Annie said.

'Well, yes, sure . . .' Ev twisted the key and unleashed the cork from its metal cage. 'But also the fact that you made it through another year. Everyone's not just surviving but thriving.' She poured two glasses of champagne.

'To thriving,' Annie said.

They clinked glasses and drank. Ev refilled them.

'Now go outside and enjoy yourself. I'll finish up in here.'

'Are you sure?' Annie asked.

'Go on.' Ev turned Annie around, undid her apron, took it off over her head, careful not to mess up her hair.

•

WHEN EV LOOKED back on it now, the toast was just one of many things she regretted from that day. That they'd clinked two glasses together and toasted to being alive. To being alive. To being alive. She thought about the year that had passed. About how different everything felt, how irreversibly changed they all were. She looked at her friends, their bodies different shapes now, their brains re-wired. The only solace she had was that they were still here. The three of them, at least, were still here. And that was something.

Twenty-three

AL PULLED UP OUTSIDE THE two-storey brick flats. He wondered if he should've called to check he was home, was up, was lucid this morning. But when Al woke he felt compelled to come here, as if coming here might fix something, might alleviate some pain – or, if not pain, some guilt.

The apartments looked shabbier than last time Al had visited. The strip of grass that divided the ground-floor flats from the footpath was dotted with the little white flowers of weeds. It needed mowing. There were wads of junk mail sticking out from the stacks of letterboxes, and an old computer monitor had been rammed into one of the small bins that sat in a row along the driveway, its screen smashed in. This place made Javeed's apartment look palatial.

Al had gone home from his drink with Nathan the night before feeling different. Not better; not yet. But with a new determination to try and get there. A new drive to patch things back together.

Crunchie had launched herself at him when he walked through the door, meowing and digging her claws into his legs through his jeans. He scooped her up and nestled his face in her ginger fur, kissed her warm body. After she'd eaten, after he'd drunk a glass of water, brushed his teeth, popped two Panadol, he let her snuggle in under his chin, let her gentle purr calm him as she kneaded at the fabric of his t-shirt. She squeaked when he held her too tight.

Claire wasn't home when he'd got there, hadn't been home while he'd been gone. She wasn't home when he woke either. He supposed she'd spent another night in the office. He hoped. He wasn't sure where else she'd go. Ev's? Perhaps the two of them stayed up too late drinking wine and Claire had slept in Ev's bed. They'd wake up hungover but together. He wouldn't text her. He wanted to give her some space. He wrote her a note, left it propped against the fruit bowl on the kitchen table, not much in it but a lemon with its zest shaved off, a browning banana.

Gone to Box Hill. Text me later. X

Now he climbed the stairs to the second floor, walked along the passage. Flats lined one side of it, the other side looked down onto a car park where two white garden chairs sat wonky on the concrete.

A venetian blind hung crooked on the inside of the front door of number six. Two slats had their ends snapped off, and if he ducked, he'd be able to peer through them. Instead, he braced himself and knocked on the glass first, then on the wood. Two sharp knocks on each. He heard movement: the shuffling of slippers on carpet, the jingling of keys turning in one lock, then another, the clanking of a chain being released, the click of the door finally being unlocked.

'Hi, Dad,' Al said. 'It's me.'

'Ali,' Hadi said, expressionless. 'Come in, come in.'

He wore a pair of navy blue flannel pyjamas, two missing buttons exposing the thick rug of white hair on his chest. The hair on his head had receded further since Al last saw him. His eyes looked watery, pink, tired.

'Did you call? I missed it, must have missed it,' Hadi said.

'I didn't, I'm sorry. I was just in the area, thought I'd drop in and see you.'

Al stepped inside the flat. At first it seemed smaller than he remembered, but then he realised there was just more stuff in there: an office chair on wheels between the armchair and the sofa, piles of newspapers and magazines stacked to knee-height along one wall. Al closed the door behind him, clicked one of the locks.

'I'll make tea.' Hadi was already shuffling to the kitchen. The shuffle was new. It might've just been the slippers. Al hoped it was just the slippers.

'Why don't I make it while you get dressed?' Al said as he moved into the kitchen.

Hadi nodded, muttered something under his breath and left the room.

Al moved some dirty plates aside and filled the kettle from the tap that shuddered and spattered before it flowed. While the water boiled, he stacked the dirty dishes on one side of the sink and found a plug, filled the basin with hot water and the last squirt of detergent from a bottle that was resting upside down, balanced delicately on its nozzle. Al made a mental note to buy his dad some dishwashing detergent.

The kettle hummed, the water rolling. Something was brewing inside Al, too. It wasn't regret. He didn't regret coming. He'd just forgotten how sad it made him. This flat, his dad's quietness.

He perused the mostly empty pantry, found a mostly empty box of teabags, placed two in the freshly washed cups and poured in the steaming water. A heaped teaspoon of sugar for his dad, another for him. Al made another note: buy more tea.

Dishes done and draining, he was dunking the teabags by the time his dad came back into the room. Hadi was dressed in a grey jumper that was full of holes: one on each elbow, one in the centre of his chest, another in the armpit.

Al had been distracted lately. It'd been too long since he'd done a clothes shop for his dad. A few shirts, underpants, jumpers, a pair of trousers.

'Your tea,' Al said, passing it to him over the kitchen bench. He could see the food stains on the sleeve of Hadi's jumper. 'After this,' he added, 'I'll go to the shops for you, Papa. Get you some food, some more tea. What else do you need?'

'Oh, nothing,' Hadi said, swatting the air as if to say, *Don't bother.*

Hadi took his cup over to the armchair next to the office chair. Al hadn't noticed, but there was a stack of boxes there too, a lamp with no bulb in it, its ceramic base cracked up the side.

'What's in the boxes, Papa?' Al asked, sitting down on the office chair. It clunked loudly and then sank slowly on its cylinder.

Hadi stared at a spot on the wall where the light snuck in through the blinds. He didn't answer Al, didn't even seem to remember he was there.

Al wished he'd got to meet the person everyone told him his father used to be. A generous man who'd only speak when he had something to say, a hard worker, dedicated to his family. But all Al remembered was Leila taking Al to visit him; the cold whiteness of the psych ward, the long quiet hours in this flat.

Hadi stood quickly, mumbled something. He left his cup cooling on the coffee table and shuffled out of the room again. Al heard drawers opening and closing in the bedroom.

Al took a sip of tea. He'd made it too strong. It was bitter, even with all that sugar. He gulped down the rest in three big mouthfuls just so it'd be over. He wanted this to be over, too. He was glad he was there but hated being there at the same time.

He hated that so often the right thing to do was the hardest, the most impossible. He thought back to his drink the previous evening, about how Nathan still wore his sadness all over him, slicked to his skin like a wetsuit. But hadn't Hadi lost more? His wife, soon after his job, his house, his mind, then his son. Al knew grief shouldn't be competitive, can't be compared. And yet he found it hard not to wonder whether it would've been easier if they'd had the same things as Nathan and Annie.

Al got out his phone; he had an hour and a half before he had to be back in Northcote. Enough time to get to the shops, to run the vacuum over the floor, to clean the fridge of mouldy food. He got to work.

AL WALKED UP and down the supermarket's wide, bright aisles. A box of Sultana Bran, a litre of milk, sachets of microwaveable rice, a box of Cup a Soup. Most of it barely food. He'd get fruit, too; maybe it'd get eaten. The red basket weighed heavy in his hand. He'd get some frozen dinners, as well: grey slabs of meat cooked god knew how long ago with a congealed gravy. His dad must be eating some of the food he bought, as the cupboards were bare of the tins of beans and the Weet-Bix from last time.

'Ali Nazari, that has to be you.' He turned to see a woman in her early sixties, brown hair pulled up in a high ponytail. 'You probably don't remember me,' she said as he studied the lines on her face as if they'd reveal her identity somehow. 'Anita Simmons.' And he saw in her his old friend's stout nose, high cheekbones. 'Jason's mum.'

'Mrs Simmons,' he said. 'Wow, of course. Sorry, it's been a while.'

'Oh, son, it's been almost twenty years. You haven't changed a bit. Beard, of course, but I'd spot you a mile off. What are you doing with yourself these days?'

'I work at SBS, on the website,' Al said.

'Ooh la la, so fancy! Good for you.' She slapped his arm. 'God, Jase will be thrilled that I bumped into you.'

Jason Simmons with that long greasy hair, with all that potential. They used to sit and sink tinnies, listen to *Nevermind* on cassette in Jason's car, the tape player advanced enough to turn itself after 'Polly'. They talked about the girls they liked, they talked about their plans for after school. Their futures were destined to be intertwined forever. Friendship felt that way at seventeen. It felt endless. But then Carmen fell off the roof and died. After it was ruled an accident, Jason, a promising footy player who stood a chance of making the AFL, just stopped playing. He refused to get out of bed to go to training, refused to get back on the field. Al had heard that he was an electrician out in Bacchus Marsh now. How did he end up in Bacchus Marsh when he was supposed to go to the AFL?

'How's he going?' Al asked.

'He's going,' Anita said, and paused. Al sensed a sadness. 'What happened to poor Carmen really put a spanner in the works for him.'

'I think that's probably true for all of us,' Al said. 'To different extents.'

'You know, I read this article the other day, so sad, about someone who died in the towers.' She made the motion of a plane flying with her hand, in case Al didn't know she meant 9/11. 'I wrote it down, hang on.' She had her handbag in the child seat of the trolley, and she fished around in it for her phone. Once found, she held her phone dramatically up to her face to unlock it, and searched around on it for ages. Al doubted the quote could be worth all this trouble. He predicted it would be the C.S. Lewis one about fear or a line from the same Maya Angelou poem that someone had written out by hand and posted anonymously to Annie. Neither of them were meaningful or helpful. He stood and waited. An Ed Sheeran song played over the loudspeaker. God, he hated Ed Sheeran. His little face popping up in *Game of Thrones*. How dare he.

'Okay, here it is, here it is.' Mrs Simmons readied herself. 'It's about grief and recovery from trauma,' she said. Al felt his face twitch. 'It says to imagine a group of people up a mountain. Except every one of them has broken bones so no one can help each other down. Everyone has to find their own way. But that assumes that everyone will make it down. The thing with trauma, with PTSD, is that some people will never make it down the

mountain at all.' Al bit his bottom lip to stop it from wobbling.
Mrs Simmons took a deep breath. 'You know, I reckon Jason
made it down that mountain, but now he's living on the other
side of it. In a different country or something.'

Her focus shifted and she stared for a few seconds into
the freezer as if she was remembering her son, remembering all the
things he could've been. She turned her attention back to Al.

'God, you had a rough trot back then, didn't you? With your
parents, then Carmen. I hope things are going well for you now.'
She said that in the same encouraging mum voice she used to
use on him back when they were teenagers. She'd always looked
out for him. She'd serve him great mounds of apricot chicken
with gluggy rice, pasta bakes made with jarred sauces, let him
and Jase go wild with the Ice Magic, squirting half a bottle each
into their bowls of vanilla ice cream. Jason's childhood, his family,
seemed idyllic to Al back then. But even that couldn't help Jason
after Carmen died. Even that couldn't bring him safely back
down the mountain.

'I'm fine, just shopping for my dad. And I'm so sorry, I've got
to get going, on a bit of a tight schedule.'

'Oh, of course, love, of course. God, it was nice seeing you,
though. I always wondered how you were doing and I'm happy
to see you're alive and well.'

'I am, thank you. It was really nice bumping into you.'

'Look, how would you feel . . .' She paused again to unlock
her phone. 'What if I give you Jason's number and maybe you

can reach out to him? I think he'd like that. I think he needs it, to be honest. Would you do that for me, love?'

There was a pleading look in her eye that Al couldn't refuse, especially after all that apricot chicken. Maybe it'd be good for both of them? Maybe it'd be horrible, stilted and awkward? Maybe it didn't matter. Al agreed. He pulled his phone from his back pocket and entered the number that Anita read out, saved it.

'Thanks, Al – you always were a good kid.'

'My pleasure. Nice seeing you, Mrs Simmons,' he said and took his basket to the checkout, unloaded it onto the conveyer belt.

ON THE SHORT drive back to his dad's he thought about Jason's number in his phone. He imagined himself staring at it for hours, thinking about ringing it. But what would he say? What would he ask? What did they have in common now except for one tragic moment they'd shared all those years ago? He worried it might be the same for him and Claire. That the only glue still binding them together was Toby. Toby's death. The deep sadness of it. How long did you have to wait to break up with someone after something like that happened? A year? He felt the panic rise in him and then remembered the little pill he'd felt in his pocket earlier. The Xanax he'd stolen from Javeed's bathroom cabinet. He parked back at his dad's, lifted his hips uncomfortably from the seat and slid a hand into his back pocket. He found the pill again. He held it up like a jeweller admiring a diamond, then he swallowed it dry. It left a powdery, chemical taste on his tongue.

Twenty-four

THEY WERE GIVEN SOCKS AT reception with little sticky pads underneath, and wristbands to unlock lockers. The three of them sat in a row unlacing their shoes, silently surveying the room. Below, in front of them, as far as the eye could see, were trampolines. Socks on, they stood and faced the black, that bouncy abyss.

'It used to be an old plane hangar,' Ev said as the opening strains of Michael Jackson's 'Beat It' thumped through the speakers.

Claire felt both hot and cold somehow. She wanted to sleep for seventeen years. She wanted to be outside in the fresh air but also cocooned in a heavy duvet. Instead she was at a 'trampoline centre'. An 'adrenaline playground'. Claire moved her head to the left, to the right, let the muscles in her neck lengthen a little. She lifted her hands above her head, her shoulders cracking, bone crunching on bone, one then two.

•

SHE'D WOKEN UP crook-necked at seven, her broken sleep interrupted by the hum of the cleaners' vacuums, by their morning chatter. She'd sat up, combed her hair with her fingers. Her breath smelled like whatever parts of the chicken they smooshed together to make the nuggets she'd wolfed down in the early hours of the morning. She thought of their pearl-pink and featherless bodies, plucked and vulnerable.

One of the cleaners knocked on her office door, asking permission to come in. Claire motioned for her to enter and sat on the sofa as she emptied the remnants of dinner from the bin, swept the vacuum across the floor around her. In her hungover state it sounded like a plane taking off.

'Thank you, miss,' the cleaner said, then she continued down the hall to the next office and the next, chatting loudly in Vietnamese to a man clearing dirty plates and mugs of cold coffee from desks and loading them onto a trolley.

Claire assessed her wounds: sore head, queasy stomach, sticky skin, stiff neck, regret. She'd live. She drank gulps of water from the drink bottle she found in her gym bag, popped the last two ibuprofen from her desk drawer. She remembered Ed's words, she remembered Janine, she remembered Helen's email, she remembered what day it was. Each one struck like a succession of piano keys playing an indiscernible tune.

She should've just caught a taxi home, thrown together some semblance of dinner from the last of the flaccid broccoli in the fridge, then replied to the last of her emails with Crunchie on her lap. She could've been fast asleep when Al stumbled home, they could've woken up together that morning. She thought back to the text she got from Helen Parkinson a month back. If only she'd ignored it. If only she'd never downloaded Tinder, never swiped right on the tall, handsome stranger; she'd never have known what it was to love someone, to truly, wholly love someone and then have them change in front of your very eyes, have everything taken away in the few minutes it took for a sweet little boy to stop breathing, for his organs to start to shut down one by one, in the time it took the ambulance to get there, to take him away. She thought about the paramedics. They were not much more than dark blue-green shapes moving through the scene, faceless to her. She wondered if they still thought about Toby, if they still thought about the scene they came barrelling into, if they still heard Annie's pleading, Nathan's sobs. She remembered one of them telling Ev that she'd done her best, that she'd done everything she could, thanking her. Ev's body shaking uncontrollably after minutes of CPR, minutes of giving him all the air in her own lungs. She remembered Annie yelling at them to wait for his socks, that he'd need his socks.

It was hard not to believe that all of it could've been avoided.

•

'WHY ARE WE doing this again?' Annie stood between them.

'Because what else were we supposed to do today?' replied Ev. 'There's not one single thing we could do today that would make sense.'

There was a family of four jumping around one corner, a small group of teenagers pushing each other over and laughing as they bounced back up. A staff member was doing somersaults and flips in the air, her body twirling in fast circles, gravity-defying, dangerous, impressive. Two people nearby were shooting basketballs into hoops, attempting slam dunks but never quite reaching, despite the extra assistance.

'I came here on a year eight excursion,' Ev yelled over the music. 'It was hell at the time, but I thought we could come one day. Maybe we could've brought Toby here when he was a bit older.'

Annie took Claire's hand in hers. Claire looked over and saw Ev on the other side of Annie, their hands joined too. Claire felt Annie's grip tighten as she counted down from three. They jumped after one and all landed at different angles on the shiny face of the trampoline. Ev jumped high and her landing sent Annie flying; she squealed as she touched down on her bum and began to laugh. Claire bounced over to her, her rhythm like that of a clumsy Neil Armstrong, and jumped one big jump right next to her. The force of Claire landing catapulted Annie up into the air as if they were on an invisible seesaw.

Ev jumped over a barrier of bright pink padding and onto a trampoline of her own. Then over another and onto another. Claire and Annie followed, spreading out across the room, jumping on different sections a few times before bounding back towards each other. They were silent as they jumped back and forth, together and then apart. Claire's head thumped but she kept jumping, compelled by something bigger to keep going.

She watched Annie jumping a few metres away. She looked like a child, lifting her knees a little too high, not quite getting the rhythm right, but with a joyful smile on her face regardless. A smile. Claire couldn't remember the last time she'd seen Annie smile, seen her laughing with her head thrown back, just like Toby used to do. Just like Toby would've done if he were here.

Claire jumped from one of the trampolines over the coloured divider and onto another. She launched herself high and put her legs out in front of her, landing on her bum and bouncing up on her feet again. Annie watched her and copied, Ev joined in too, and the three of them bounced from their feet to their bums and back again for a few minutes. Three adult women locked in this strange ritual, this mourning dance.

Ev broke first, stumbled sweating to the padding between the black.

'Oh my god,' she said, breathless. 'I am so unfit.' She bent over, hands on hips.

Claire bounced beside her and stepped onto the mat, the sensation of firm ground beneath her socked feet suddenly strange. She'd become used to the trampoline's give, its stretch.

Ev breathed deeply. She wiped her forehead with her forearm, wiped her forearm on her t-shirt.

They stood and watched Annie fall onto her knees and bounce back up to her feet.

'She looks' – Claire paused – 'sort of happy?'

'I didn't know if we'd ever see it again.' Ev was shaking her head with wonder.

Claire thought back to the last time she'd seen Annie happy. It was the night of Toby's birthday, the last twenty minutes of his life.

•

THEY WERE SITTING outside in the warm November evening. Ev in the corner spraying herself with insect repellent, the mosquitoes out for blood. Annie had lit citronella candles. Claire would never forget that smell. It made her feel sick now; she'd rather get eaten alive than smell it again.

'An excellent party, Annabelle,' Claire said, and they all gave her a round of applause. Annie stood and took a bow, flopped back down on the cushions they'd pulled off the outdoor furniture.

'I'm so tired,' Annie said. 'But it was good, wasn't it? I think he liked it.'

'Are you kidding?' Ev said. 'He loved it. He's a Woodward, he loves being the centre of attention.'

Ev ducked as Nathan threw a salt-and-vinegar chip at her.

'Hey, so I have a little congratulations-on-surviving-two-years-of-parenthood present for you two,' Al said. He pulled a gift-wrapped box out his shirt pocket. 'I was going to give it to you earlier, but it didn't seem appropriate with the visiting dignitaries.'

Al stood and presented the box to Annie on two outstretched hands, his head bowed. Annie grinned, rattled it. Al smiled at Claire. He looked so proud of himself. He looked so at home here, her friends now firmly his too.

'Do you want to do the honours?' Annie said, holding it out to Nathan, who sat cross-legged at the edge of the group.

'All yours,' he said, and they watched her lift the sticky tape from the paper, unfold the edges. She slid the gift out of its wrapper. It was a matchbox.

'Wow,' she said, smiling, tipsy and sweet enough to think this was the best present ever.

Al laughed. 'Open it, silly.'

She slid the box from its casing. Ev stood to peer in.

'Oh my god,' Annie said. She reached into the little box and pulled out a joint. She giggled. 'Al!'

She smelled it and screwed up her nose. Ev laughed and clapped.

'Do you know, I have never smoked pot before in my life,' Annie said.

'That doesn't surprise me in the slightest,' said Al. 'Now's as good a time to start as any.'

'What if I become addicted?' Annie said, serious suddenly. 'I can't start watching Seth Rogen movies now. I'm thirty-five.'

'I promise we'll intervene if it gets that bad,' Claire said, putting an arm around the back of Al's chair, her hand falling on his shoulder.

'We'll keep an eye on your Netflix account,' Ev said.

'You're not going to get addicted from one joint, I promise,' Al assured her as Annie turned the joint in her hand.

'Can we?' Annie looked at Nathan.

The rest of them turned to face him too, as if he was everyone's dad.

'You can do what you like,' he said, smiling at her encouragingly. 'But I probably have to go to Canberra in the morning.'

Just as he said it, his phone rang – a loud urgent ring, like an alarm bell. He smiled an *I'm sorry* smile, a *Please forgive me* smile, and stood to go into the house.

'If that's who I think it is, tell him sovereignty was never ceded,' Ev yelled after him. 'And that we need a treaty and we need it now.'

'You do know that that ringtone does actually mean it's someone important,' Annie said, her eyes wide.

Ev smiled conspiratorially.

'So, are we doing this?' Al asked, holding up a cigarette lighter.

Annie looked around the circle of her friends and nodded enthusiastically.

•

CLAIRE COULDN'T TELL if the throbbing was the music or her head. She felt unsteady on her feet. She closed her eyes.

'How's that hangover?' Ev asked. She put her arm around Claire's waist to steady her. Claire let herself be held, be held up.

'It's back with a vengeance,' Claire said.

'Hey,' Ev said without missing a beat, 'I just wanted to check' – she squeezed Claire tighter, looked up at her – 'are you okay?'

Claire looked back at her, felt a tide building inside her. She opened her mouth to say no but before she could, Annie came bounding towards them.

'Come on, we're going over there.' She pointed at two long, narrow trampolines, at the end of which were pits filled with soft spongey bricks. They looked like runways.

Claire and Ev stood at one end and watched Annie bunny hop down to the other. She stopped just before the pit and jumped, throwing herself sideways into it.

She shrieked with childlike joy, let out a laugh that sounded just like Toby's.

'Come on!' Annie called. She was trying to pull herself upright but kept sinking into the foam, laughing through the struggle.

'I'm coming,' Ev yelled. She took six big jumps and on the seventh curled her body and jumped like a cannonball into the pit.

'Wooo!' Annie clapped, still submerged in foam. Ev crawled out of the pit to make way for Claire.

'Come on, Claire, you can do it!' Annie yelled.

Claire stepped onto the trampoline and jumped down towards the pit, trying to jump high and land clean, with enough pace that she could launch herself once she got to the end. But her body seemed to take on a new momentum, her boobs going at one speed, her stomach at another; her legs had a life of their own. She bounced to the very end of the long black strip and realised she'd misjudged the distance. She landed too close to the end. Without the trampoline or momentum left to jump again she panicked and stepped forward, falling ungracefully, face first, into the foam.

She rolled over and heard Annie cackling beside her. She lifted her head up and couldn't help but smile through the embarrassment.

Annie was on her back, red-faced from laughing so hard. 'That was the best thing I've ever seen,' she said breathlessly. 'Thank you.'

Ev was laughing on the other side of her, bending over, holding her stomach.

'I did it on purpose just for your amusement.' Claire looked around to see if anyone else had seen her fall, but no one was watching. No one cared.

'You're a true friend,' Annie said, wiping the tears from her eyes, catching her breath. Then suddenly, 'Shit, shit, help me up.'

'What?'

'I need to pee,' Annie said. '*Quick!*' She motioned for them both to come to her.

Ev stepped over onto Annie's trampoline and tried to jog over to her, but instead she wobbled, the motion throwing her balance off. She landed on her knees, got back on her feet, took a step forward, wobbled again and fell on her arse.

Annie howled, rolling back and forth like a cartoon of someone laughing.

'Oh god, I – I just weed a little,' she said. 'Shit.'

Ev laughed then too.

'Help, help, help. Stop laughing and help!' Annie was giggling while trying to pull herself up.

Ev steadied herself and held a hand out, Claire reached over too and they managed to pull Annie up and out of the pit.

'Go, go,' Ev said, and Annie started jogging towards the toilets.

Claire and Ev followed. By the time they got there, Annie was already sighing with relief.

'Oh my god,' Annie said. 'That was a close one.'

The three of them sat in adjacent stalls, the only sound the gentle tinkle of piss hitting water.

'I went on a date last night,' Claire heard Ev say from the stall to her right.

'Why didn't you tell us?' Claire asked. Just a few hours ago Ev'd said that she'd stayed home, watched TV. Was she embarrassed? 'Is it someone we know?'

'It's not Fred, is it?' Annie asked. There was the rustle of toilet paper. 'You can tell us if it is.'

'Oh my god, no,' Ev said. 'It's no one you know. I didn't say anything because I thought you might think it's weird to go on a date the night before' – Ev paused – 'you know.'

'It's no more weird than coming here,' Claire said, and they all laughed quietly.

Claire thought of what Ev had said earlier. What else were they supposed to do today? Visit his grave, give speeches, grow, heal. She remembered what Al had told her about the ethos behind *Seinfeld*, his favourite show. 'No hugging, no learning.'

'It went well, though,' Ev said. 'And that's all I'm going to say about the matter at this time.'

'I had a job interview in Sydney yesterday,' Claire said before she could stop herself. There were audible gasps from the stalls either side of her. 'With Helen Parkinson. She's mounting a huge class action on behalf of some teenagers to stop the government approving a new coal mine.'

'Whoa,' Ev said. 'That's – that's huge.'

'Teenagers?' Annie asked.

'The argument is that it will harm young people by exacerbating climate change.'

'Whoa,' Ev said again. 'That's fucking cool.'

'I haven't got it yet. But I think they'll make an offer.' It felt good talking about it. It was easier to say out loud when she couldn't see their faces, the sadness or disappointment. It felt like confession, only smellier.

'It sounds like your dream job,' Ev said.

'Yeah,' Claire said, and it was. Finally she had a chance to actually make a difference to the world on a big scale, to really *do* something with her life that was meaningful. It was seeing Toby, knowing Toby, that really cemented the dream for her. She had wanted the world to be better for him.

'What does Al think?' Ev asked. The question felt like a knee in the guts.

'I haven't told him yet,' Claire said and she winced.

She heard a sharp intake of breath on either side of her.

'Things' – Claire felt her lip wobble – 'things have been hard lately. I've been burying myself in work, hardly home. It's like we're housemates or on different planets or something. And . . . I think Al's drinking too much.' Tears slid silently down her cheek. She used a few squares of the scratchy toilet paper to catch them, dry them. She blew her nose.

'Oh, Claire bear,' Annie said sadly.

Claire hated it when Annie called her that, but she couldn't tell her now. Now, she'd let Annie call her anything she wanted.

'You just need to talk to each other,' Ev said hopefully. 'You still love each other, right? That's enough to get through it.'

'We do,' Claire said. 'I still love him more than anything.' But the truth was she had no idea if he felt much other than irritated, hungover.

'What about you, Annie?' Ev said. 'Anything you want to talk about?'

Annie laughed but it sounded defeated, hollow.

'I don't even know where to start,' Annie said. 'Except that I miss him with my whole body. So much so that sometimes I think I want to die too.'

'Annie, no,' Ev and Claire cried in unison.

'No, it's okay. I don't really mean it. I could never do that to Nathan, to you guys.'

Claire didn't know what to say; she didn't know how to allay Annie's fears. Ev stayed quiet too. She heard one of the others sniff, thick and snotty.

'I always thought we'd take him to Disneyland. I imagined his first day at school, what he'd be like as a big brother, his wedding. I had my whole life planned around him and now I don't know what to do with myself. I'm lost.'

'You're not lost,' Ev said. 'You're here with us. We'll work our way through it together. Okay?'

Claire didn't know how Ev always knew the right thing to say but she was glad for it. She imagined how they'd look from above: the three of them sitting with their pants down crying in the stalls of the women's toilet at Bounce. She smiled.

The door to the bathroom opened and brought with it the loud music from outside. Two voices groaned at the occupied stalls. Claire flushed, heard the other two do the same. She pulled up her leggings, took a deep breath and readied herself to meet her friends at the mirror.

As she opened the door, a teenage girl barrelled past her for the toilet.

'Don't mind her – we're a bit hungover,' the other girl, dressed in baggy nineties-style jeans and a crop top, said. She could've been Claire twenty years ago (not too far off Claire now – trampolining with a stinking hangover). The girl shuffled into the cubicle after her friend, presumably to hold her hair, rub her back. All the things friends do for each other.

She and Annie and Ev stood at the sinks, all three of them puffy-eyed, their cheeks tear-streaked. Claire washed her hands, dried them on her pants. She felt her socks absorb liquid from the floor.

'I love you guys,' Ev said and put her arms around Annie.

'I love you too,' Annie said.

Claire stepped towards them, put an arm around each of them, and they stood and held on to each other for dear life.

'I WANT TO try the basketball one,' Annie said when they were back outside in the plane hangar.

'Didn't you just almost wet yourself?' Ev asked.

'It was only a little one,' Annie said.

'I'm going to sit this one out,' Claire said and plonked herself down on a nearby bench.

'I'll take one for the team,' Ev whispered and followed Annie back down onto the mats and over to two basketball hoops ringed by tall nets.

Claire watched them play. Annie running and readying herself for a slam dunk, but when she jumped her feet barely left the ground. She lobbed the ball but it didn't even hit the hoop. Ev tried next, running, jumping and wobbling and then shooting from a stationary point like a netball player. The ball bounced twice on the top of the ring and slid in through the net. Annie yelled, high-fived her.

Claire smiled. What would happen if she left this? What would happen to her if she left Al? If they left together? There were too many unanswerable questions, there were too many unknowns. She wasn't sure she could do this to them. She wasn't sure she could do it at all. She pulled her phone from the pocket of her leggings. She opened her email.

She swiped right on Helen's email and deleted it.

EV DROVE THEM down the freeway, then back through the suburbs. They drove past new apartment blocks that shimmered silver and white, past squat brick bungalows. Each one of them the centre of someone's universe, each one of them the scene of some kind of crime.

Annie sat quietly in the passenger seat, facing straight ahead, her head unmoving. It was as if she could only focus on what was right in front of her. There was no back or sideways, only onwards.

Claire was sitting in the back seat, her head resting against the window. Her seatbelt felt tight across her chest. She turned her phone over and over in her hand. It felt lighter now the email was gone. She wished the other things could be altered so easily. A swipe and the funny, kind, thoughtful Al would come back. A swipe and Toby would come back. She felt exhausted, the tiredness hanging around her head like fog on a mountain range, the colour of seagulls, of storm clouds, her grandfather's hair.

In the front, Ev turned on the radio. Claire knew how much she hated silence, how it weighed her down. She often couldn't even ride her bike the fifteen minutes to work without her headphones in, a podcast on.

The first station was a traffic update: a three-car pile-up on the Ring Road, a car flipped on the Western Freeway, a report on the worst day of someone's life, on someone else's misery.

Ev used the buttons on the steering wheel to flick between stations. An easy listening station was playing 'Tears in Heaven'.

'No! Next!' Claire screamed as soon as she recognised it.

'Way too sad,' Ev said. She flicked past a Green Day song and some angry talkback.

'This,' Annie said. 'This is perfect.' They all recognised the opening strains of 'Walk Like an Egyptian'. Annie started singing along. She knew every word.

'The lyrics to this song are nonsense,' Claire said. She'd never really listened to them properly before. There was a bit about crocodiles and cigarettes, blonde waitresses.

'Is it maybe a bit racist?' Ev asked.

'A simplistic interpretation of a rich and complex ancient culture, that's for sure,' Claire said.

'Don't ruin this for me,' Annie said. Claire watched Annie as she started doing the dance from the video clip with her hands.

Ev made eye contact with Claire in the rear-view mirror, her thick eyebrows raised. Claire smiled at her, and both of them joined in for the chorus, for the wheeeey-ohs.

Claire thought back to all the times Annie had made them go to karaoke, how she'd always dominated the microphone, picked the hardest songs for herself and sung them word perfect but pitch oblivious, mostly without looking at the lyrics on the screen. Claire dreaded every session; the only enjoyable part about it for someone who didn't know the verse to any song, couldn't hold a tune and couldn't read fast enough to keep up with the screen, was watching Annie sing.

The opening strains of 'Africa' by Toto came on the radio and Annie shrieked with recognition.

'Is this racist-song Saturday on Gold FM?' Claire asked.

'Don't you ruin this for me,' Annie said again and started crooning.

'Apparently they play this instead of a bell at the primary school up the road,' Ev said. 'There's going to be thousands of kids with a Pavlovian response to this song.'

'A terrifying future for our world,' Claire said, shaking her head. It felt almost like normal, this car trip back through the suburbs. Almost.

Claire's stomach rumbled audibly. She hadn't eaten anything since the chicken nuggets, since the vomiting.

'I'm starving,' she said over Annie's singing. 'I think I'd like to eat yum cha. Or noodles. Or pho. Or pizza?'

'When will Nath be home?' Ev asked, indicating, changing lanes.

'Soon, I hope,' Annie said.

'So I bought some food on my way over today,' Ev said, without taking her eyes off the road. 'It's some of Toby's favourite foods. What I could find at the supermarket, anyway.'

'Ev,' Annie said, and then nothing else.

From the back seat, Claire could hear her sniffling.

'Home then?' Annie said.

'Home,' Claire said and opened her phone, opened her email, scrolled down to the trash. *Looking good. Looking good.* She thought about what Ev said from the toilet stall. It *was* fucking cool. She swiped the email again, moved it back into her inbox, put her phone face down.

Claire reached a hand over the back of the seat and squeezed Annie's shoulder. Annie put her hand on Claire's and they sat like that, their fingers entwined, all the way home.

Twenty-five

NATHAN WAITED IN THE CAR at the end of the driveway. He hadn't really thought this through. Not properly. He couldn't remember the last time he was able to see clearly.

On the drive over, he'd convinced himself that if he apologised, it would change something. It would make something right. But what? He'd just go back to walking on eggshells around her, go back to letting his parents dominate his life. In his darkest moments, he imagined selling the house and giving them back the money they'd given him and Annie as a wedding present. But then where would they live? In a house without his son's fingerprints, in a house containing no evidence that he'd ever existed.

It was exactly three years since Toby was born, a year after Toby had died. A tiny person capable of turning their lives inside out and upside down again and again.

Nathan thought about his little body. This time not about the oxygen disappearing from his blood, from his brain, but about the deep, lake-blue of his eyes, rimmed by thick lashes, the little red birthmark behind his ear, the xylophone bones of his ribs. How was he gone? How?

•

IT HAD BEEN hard leaving Annie that morning, when she was awake early for the first time in a year. They'd eaten breakfast together – freezer toast, butter, peanut butter, one of her pieces with a smear of honey, the last squeeze from a plastic bottle, its corners packed with dark, crystallised sugar. She used the machine to make them coffee; the grinding, the steaming, the sounds of routine were comforting. It was hard not to feel as though they were performing a well-learned ritual from before.

'I can be there and back in an hour,' Nathan had told her.

He watched her tongue move as she tried to dislodge the thick film of peanut butter attached to the roof of her mouth. The soft pink of her lips, of her tongue – it stirred something in him.

'You know you don't have to go,' she said.

'I know, but I also do,' he said, and she nodded. 'I'm sorry it's today, though; sorry it's now.'

'Me too,' she said.

'What will you do this morning?' he asked.

'I suspect Ev will make an appearance at some point,' she said. 'She's so good to us.'

'She is,' Annie agreed. 'Maybe we'll do something later, all of us?'

'Ev asked me about that yesterday,' he said, putting the dry crusts back on his plate. He couldn't stomach the last of them. He imagined having people around. 'What, though?'

'I'll think about it,' she said. 'Text you if I come up with anything.'

'I just can't make a speech or anything,' he said. The thought of it, of keeping it together, of finding the right words. How did one describe a giant black hole, the absence of things, the suspension of time?

'No one will expect that.'

Maybe Bob and Cherie would, but they wouldn't be invited. He was surprised they hadn't suggested a formal memorial service, a marquee event in their backyard with photos of Toby blown up to A2 size and dotted around on easels, trays of canapés passed around. The two of them play acting like the grieving grandparents, putting on a show.

•

NATHAN LET THE engine idle as he imagined turning up the driveway, parking, going inside, apologising to his mother. He wrote a script in his head. It would be easy to memorise his lines, but he knew their delivery wouldn't be believable. He pressed the ignition button and the engine quietened. He knew he should get out but he couldn't. He couldn't get his hands to unfasten his seatbelt, his legs to walk him up the drive. Annie was right: he didn't have to go. He owed them nothing. He owed nothing to anyone. Except Toby. Only Toby. He turned the car back on, drove slowly to the end of the cul-de-sac, turned around and drove too quickly past the house again.

He kept driving: down to the end of the street and then left, right onto the main road, onto the highway. Driving away from the city, away from his parents, away from his home, his wife, the body of his dead son that would just be bones now. The thought of that like a knife in the guts.

The further he drove, the further he'd be from the guilt, from the pain.

His phone hummed from its spot in the centre console, the glass screen vibrating against the plastic of the cup holder. He ignored it. It was probably a well-wisher, someone with some words of consolation or affirmation. The platitudes he'd heard over the last year were so similar he'd wondered how many of the people in his life had gone online and searched for 'what to say to a bereaved parent'.

There was nothing to be said! No words that could ever make it better, easier, make it not have happened.

All he wanted was for it not to have happened.

After Toby died, after the hospital, the police, the forms, and that first night when they both took sleeping pills and woke up four hours later and were forced to remember again, after the funeral – all that was left was time. Empty hours in which Nathan was alive and Toby was not. Time which he should be using for something important, something valuable, something to honour his son's life, something to make it meaningful. But instead he spent his time with his head in the sand, putting down card after card in his games of solitaire.

He drove further and further, onto a highway and then off. If he just kept driving, maybe he'd get far enough away to find some peace.

HE PULLED INTO a parking spot. Nearby, sulphur-crested cocka-toos crowded a picnic table as they searched for crumbs, their yellow crests like a lick of cartoon hair. A few bright red rosellas bounced around between them.

The road east from his parents' house climbed and wound up and up, the trees changing from big plane trees to roadside grevilleas planted by councils, their pointed leaves and alien-head flowers in bright pink, the colour of a tropical cocktail. Higher up, giant tree ferns fanned over valleys; above them, mountain ash towered with their tall, white trunks revealed by bark that seemed to be peeling itself off like skin.

Out of the car, the air smelled of eucalyptus, of damp forest. It felt thinner, better. He stood and watched the birds, their cries echoing through the sky.

He walked back down the road a little, past the cafe where a few tourists sat on the deck eating sandwiches, drinking cappuccinos that, he could tell from the smell of the beans in the air, tasted burnt, bitter.

He took the path near the wide dirt track. The sun shone through the high canopy. He looked up. The tops of the trees seemed to form a crown around the forest, the tips of their branches not touching. He'd read about this once. That some trees grow like this on purpose; they sense the other trees there and stay apart to protect each other.

The bird calls across the forest were cacophonous; the accusatory laughs of the kookaburras, the squawks and hoots of others he didn't recognise.

He forged on, uphill on wet leaves, past a downed trunk that lay collapsed across the forest floor, life carrying on around it, regrowing despite it. This felt meaningful to him there in the fresh air, in the warmth of the day.

Around a corner, down another valley, he'd been walking for half an hour, then an hour. He was thirsty but it didn't matter. He kept going. There were sprays of mud coming up the sides of his white sneakers, but he didn't care. He just cared about the forest. He wondered if this was what would heal him: these tall trees, the mossy logs, the ancient, Jurassic Park tree ferns with shaggy hair sprouting from their bases, their bright green fronds spread out like the wings of eagles in flight. All these colours. He hadn't known there were so many different greens.

He stopped and sat on the dirt bank into which the path was cut. He'd been walking for an hour and a half. He felt invigorated. He felt hungry. Behind him, he heard the leaves rustle. He turned to see a bird, its body a dull grey but its tail an exquisite span of white and brown feathers. Its call sounded like a mash-up of other bird sounds, of a toy laser gun firing, of a mobile phone ringing, of a kookaburra, a nail gun – the bird cycled through them, seeming not to take a breath.

'Hello, bird,' he said quietly, so as not to alarm it.

The lyrebird squawked and hollered in response.

He wanted it to speak. If he were in a film or a book, the bird would speak to him. The bird would have come to him with a message. It would forgive him, it would bury his grief in its nest, it would set him free.

But he knew the bird was just a bird. It shook its little brown body, it kicked at the leaf litter on the forest floor.

Nathan stood, edged past it and jogged down the track a little. He laughed at the thought of it, of this bird speaking to him, of this bird healing him, making him whole.

He laughed as he picked up the pace, almost running now on the slippery leaf-covered path. He skidded a few times in muddy patches, jumped over puddles. He imagined landing arse-first in a patch of mud and that made him laugh even more. Toby would've loved that, he thought, would've laughed very hard at that. He was running properly now, his lungs hot. He passed a young family, a small tour group of retirees. They all stopped in their tracks as he bolted past, his maniacal laugh echoing across the valley. He imagined the bird mimicking him, too.

He ran out into the car park and stopped dead in his tracks. He was breathless, sweating. He leaned over, his hands on his knees, as he got his breath back. A few people gave him sideways glances, raised an eyebrow. He must've looked a sight: the back of his shirt wet, armpits swampy, but he felt exhilarated, alive. He was alive. That was a miracle.

He went to the cafe and bought a cup of tea, a pre-made ham-and-cheese sandwich: just a stripe of yellow and a stripe of pink on slightly stale white bread. A sunset of a sandwich.

He took it to one of the picnic tables, the birds far away, seeking food elsewhere, and ate quickly, quietly. He could hear his chewing inside his head, like a washing machine. He swallowed loudly, the mechanism of swallowing so natural to him. He felt the food travel down his throat, imagined it making its way to his stomach. Swallowing shouldn't be a thing that can kill you, he thought. That just doesn't seem fair. But then your heart can stop beating for no reason, your blood can coagulate and move through your body, get to your brain and clog things up. Cells can take over and eat each other and your blood can poison you and your lungs can fail and you can just fall over dead at any point so why not swallowing, why not. His hand shook as he drank his tea, milky with a tiny bit of sugar, steaming hot and calming. He sat at the table, watched the birds, watched the trees dance in the gentle wind. He smelled the forest and felt okay, stronger or something. Back in the car, his phone sat still in its plastic cup holder, a screen full of notifications. He decided to leave it there. He left the radio off, he started the car and he headed for home.

Twenty-six

ANNIE SAT ON THE GRASS in the backyard. She felt different; her whole body looser, her mind clearer. Maybe she'd get a trampoline installed in the garden. Maybe she'd give every room of the house a trampoline for a floor. If that was what it took.

She looked at her friends; Claire lay with an arm over her eyes shielding her hangover from the sun. Ev had put out a spread: Cheezels, carrot sticks, hummus, grapes. She'd opened a bottle of wine and sat with a mug of it watching birds jump around in the trees.

'Can we do fun things more often?' Annie asked. Claire tilted her head, moved her arm to look at her, she squinted as if trying to focus.

'I'll make a list,' Ev said.

'I'd like to go on a rollercoaster,' Annie said.

'We can make that happen,' Claire sat up, smiled at her. 'What about roller skating?'

'Writing it down,' Ev said, typing into her phone. 'I think there's pirate-themed mini-golf on the way to Philip Island.'

Annie nodded. She felt a warmth rising in her. She ate a Cheezel. She wanted to fill herself up with life, with fun. Maybe that's the only thing to do when someone dies. Live more life. Live the most amount of life possible. She licked the neon orange dust from her fingers.

Twenty-seven

'THINGS HAVE BEEN HARD LATELY,' Al said, summoning all his courage. 'Exactly a year ago my friend's son died and it's bringing up a lot of grief from my past. I think I need some help . . . a mental health plan.'

It felt good to say it aloud, good to be doing something about it. He wanted to text Zahra and tell her, wanted her to be proud, to forgive him.

'That sounds like a very shitty year,' the doctor said.

From a drawer, she pulled out a clipboard and passed it to him. On it, a K10 test, a list of feelings. She asked him to rate how frequently he'd experienced them in the last four weeks.

How often had he felt tired out for no good reason?

How often did he feel nervous?

How often had he felt so restless he could not sit still?

He saw all his ticks skewing towards the right-hand side of the page.

Most of the time.

Some of the time.

Most of the time.

He passed the form back to the doctor and looked around the room of the fancy Northcote clinic as she assessed his answers: a devil's ivy snaked across a bookshelf; a model of a human heart, its left ventricle exposed; books about cancer, one about lupus, a library of all the things that could go wrong, things that we couldn't control.

'You've scored quite high for anxiety and depression,' she said, looking at him. Her grey hair was cut short. A practical haircut for a busy woman. Maybe she liked how little maintenance was involved, how quick it was to dry. Maybe she liked the feeling of the wind against her neck.

'Have you had any thoughts about ending your life?' she asked in her crisp doctorly way, not without feeling but without condescension, without pity. Al liked her.

'No, none at all.'

'Good. Sleep?'

'Interrupted but okay,' he said. 'Could be better, could be worse.'

She nodded.

'I'm probably drinking a bit too much,' he said shyly. Then, more bravely, 'Not probably: definitely.'

She nodded again. Didn't lecture him, didn't ask any more questions. She just gave him options: a referral to a psychiatrist, a psychologist with ten appointments subsidised by Medicare, a prescription for fluoxetine, a small amount of hope, a follow-up appointment in three weeks, a promise that things would get easier, that talking about it, doing something about it, was good, important. That he was right to come in and see her when he did.

OUT IN THE sunshine, he stretched his arms above his head and headed for the pharmacy. He did feel different. Maybe it was the Xanax, or maybe it was that he felt momentum, he felt a modicum of control. He wanted to walk in the warm sun, he wanted to eat a banh mi, he wanted to see Claire, was desperate to see Claire, to talk to her, to hold her, to put everything back together and make it right. To apologise for how he'd been behaving. He felt so ashamed.

'Don't put a hat on a hat,' Ev had said to him once. He'd looked at her, puzzled, and she explained: 'If you feel bad about something, just let yourself feel bad about it. Don't feel bad for feeling bad. You'd never put a hat on a hat.'

'Where did you get that from?' Al asked her.

'I saw it on Instagram.'

'Oh my god,' Al said, laughing.

'It was from a book originally!' Ev said defensively. 'I just don't know which one.'

He'd made fun of her that day, but the saying had stayed with him, and now he stopped himself from feeling guilty. He just let himself feel.

He got out his phone to text Claire, but she'd beaten him to it.

Come to Nathan and Annie's? We'll all be there. Xx

Al dropped his prescription in at the pharmacy, stood in the vitamin aisle and read the names on the bottles while he waited for it to be filled. He replayed that morning, when he'd come back with the shopping.

He'd stacked the cans of baked beans and the microwave rice sachets in the cupboard. He'd cleaned some almost-liquid vegetables from the crisper in the fridge. He'd said, 'I have to go now, Papa,' and Hadi said nothing, barely moved, his attention focused elsewhere, on nothing in particular that Al could see. When Al went over to say goodbye, Hadi looked up, seeming surprised Al was there in the flat at all. Al hugged him, and, through his holey jumper, had felt his skin and bones.

A young woman called Al's name. She held the box of pills, asked him if he'd had the medication before, gave him a few photocopied, stapled pieces of paper about side effects when he said he hadn't. He carried it all to the front counter. He'd read it later. He almost didn't care. No side effect could be worse than how he'd been feeling the last few weeks, the last twelve months. Longer? He didn't even know anymore. He was sure there were times when he was happy. When he'd felt clear-headed, when he had the capacity for joy. The trip to Europe he took with Claire. When he'd held Toby over his head, swung him around, heard the boy's screams of pure delight, his guttural giggles. Waking up next to Claire on mornings when she didn't leave for work early, her arm reaching across his chest, a foot wedged between calves. He could get it back, he knew he could. He had to.

AL SAW THE mess of the garden from the gate. He stood stock-still, caught off guard by it. Upset by the state of it. It felt like a metaphor for their lives, for their year. The piles of dying plants, the holes from which they'd been ripped. They were the dying plants. Toby was the empty holes, the absence of what was once perfect.

He rang the doorbell, heard footsteps down the hall. He was expecting Nathan or Annie to open the door, to hug him. He'd practised what he'd say on the drive over. A version of, *I'm so sorry,* or, *I miss him.* Or, *We made it* (but had they?). Instead it was Claire at the door. She looked tired, crumpled. She was in gym clothes. She had dark bags under her eyes. He'd never been so happy to see her. So relieved. He tried to speak, to say some of the things he wanted to say, but before he could, she collapsed into him.

He put his arms around her and she cried onto his shoulder. Through his t-shirt, he felt her tears on his skin.

'I'm sorry,' she whispered into his neck.

'No, I'm sorry,' he said, and that made her cry more, cry harder. She pulled back from him, wiped her cheeks.

'Let's get through today,' he said, putting a hand on each of her bony shoulders, squeezing them. 'And then let's talk. I'm here now, okay. And I'm not going anywhere.'

Claire wiped her face with the sleeve of her top. He waited while she ducked into the hall bathroom, blew her nose, splashed water on her cheeks, tried to calm the redness of her eyes. Then he let her take his hand and lead him into the house.

He dropped her hand when they got to the kitchen. He walked past it, past the spot where it'd happened, and stood over the other side of the marble bench while she took a beer from the fridge. He still couldn't bear to look at it, still found it hard to move around in the space. The place where Toby died.

It always came back to him in flashes. At first, multiple times a day. At work when he was sending emails, or in meetings, on the train, on the tram, at the pool when he'd dip his head below surface, the water making everything blue, making reality abstract, making it wobble and wave. He'd see Toby's legs sticking out from behind the counter, Nathan standing over him screaming.

The intensity and frequency of the flashbacks lessened over time, but still they were there. And often, along with the memory of Toby's face, and the sounds of crying, of screaming, came the memory of Carmen's face, the sound of the metal below her cracking, the sight of her body crooked on the ground. Both times, the slow sad boredom at the hospital as they waited for confirmation of what they already knew. The unspeakable words that had to be said. Toby was dead. Carmen was dead.

He'd been the one who called the ambulance this time. The call ringing and ringing and ringing, until finally someone answered. He gave the postcode or something close to it.

'Ambulance,' he said. 'Ambulance. Ambulance. He's not breathing, please hurry.'

He recited the address, handed his phone to Nathan to answer the questions the operator was asking. Al had never thought about what those questions might've been. Does he have a pulse? Is he breathing? Can you clear his airway? How old is he? What's his name? What colour are his lips? Why is this happening to you? Why?

He remembered Nathan screaming answers down the phone, he remembered the sound coming out of Annie. Not screams so much as screeches, untamed, wild, already knowing, her body comprehending before the rest of her, before the rest of them.

Annie and Nathan got in the ambulance, someone called an Uber, and they ran into the hospital waiting room, running as if their speed could affect something. As if there'd be anything for them to do once they got there. They just waited. Claire went to the cafeteria and bought some sandwiches, and then they just sat on plastic chairs, sat on narrow hospital sofas, and waited, until Nathan came out to tell them that Toby was dead, Toby had died, and he almost fell as he told them. Al saw his knees buckle and caught him before he fell and then Ev held him up as he cried, and Ev cried, and Al was sure she was saying sorry, sorry, again and again.

Al's phone had been left behind at the house and they only found it hours later when he and Claire and Ev went to tidy up. Nathan and Annie spent the night at the hospital, either in with Toby or pacing the halls or dozing uncomfortably in seats not made for sleep. Annie and Nathan's parents had arrived. Al found out later that Ev had called them, that she had somehow strung the words together to make full sentences, while Al and Claire sat comatose and useless. She was a wonder, Ev. A strong, funny, beautiful wonder of a woman.

He heard her laugh from the garden and turned to see Annie and Ev sitting on the grass. Being there, it felt as if the day Toby died was a movie he'd seen once.

Claire opened his beer, brought it around the bench to him. He sipped it and watched her.

'Can you believe it was a year ago?' she asked.

'Not really. But it also feels like ten years.'

'I know,' she said. 'He'd only be three today.' She looked as though she was about to cry again, whispered: 'I really loved him.'

Al put his arm around Claire and kissed her forehead, then bent down to kiss her mouth. She put a hand on his cheek as she kissed him back.

OUT ON THE lawn, three blankets were spread on the grass. Above them, the sky wide, blue, empty of clouds and birds, the sun heading out of view. Here they were – four of them, at least – back in this spot a year later. They had made it down the mountain.

Al sat with his long legs in front of him. The sun felt good on his face. Next to him was a plate of party pies and sausage rolls, cold now but they'd been warmed in the oven by Ev. Ants were marching purposefully around the dipping bowl of sauce that was flecked with lost pastry.

They were still sitting on the grass when Nathan arrived. He seemed different to last night: slightly giddy, his energy off kilter. He walked out onto the grass barefoot.

Annie got up to greet him and Al watched them kiss, watched him hug her tenderly, whisper something into her ear that made her lips curve slightly, a barely perceptible smile but a smile all the same. A welcome sight.

Ev stood, wrapped her arms around him and the two of them hugged.

Nathan hugged Al next, came to where he sat and bent right over, the two of them slapping each other's backs, not mentioning last night. It was nice not to. It was nice to have a thing that was just theirs. Nathan kissed the top of Claire's head, squeezed her shoulder.

Toby would've loved them all being there like this. He would've run around between them, initiating high fives, ruining knock-knock jokes because he hadn't yet understood how they worked, laughing so hard he'd fall over. Once so hard he farted. Al smiled thinking of him. The memories physically hurt. It didn't seem fair that they'd never make new ones. He wondered if Carmen's parents felt the same. If they'd made it down the mountain at all.

'Have you shown them the book?' Nathan asked Annie once he'd sat down beside her.

'I haven't, I'll get it.' Annie jumped up and jogged inside.

'How was Cherie today?' Ev asked Nathan before pulling the flesh off a slice of orange until all that was left was pith and skin.

'Ah, I didn't make it,' Nathan said, but before anyone could ask questions, Annie walked back out onto the deck: two beers under each arm, the bottle opener between her teeth, a scrapbook in one hand.

Ev jumped up, grabbed the book, let Annie drop the bottle opener from her mouth into Ev's hand. With fresh drinks – just this last one, Al thought, and then I'm done, then I'm done – they crowded around the book. Ev was crying before she even opened the cover. The book had been gifted to them, Nathan explained, by Ruby. There were rainbows, a sun on which gold glitter had been stuck, colourful flowers. The photo on the cover was a group shot. Fran and Tess had their arms around each other, Tess's dark hair piled high on her head, freckles covering the bridge of her nose; Fran beaming, surrounded by her family. Ruby had her hands on Toby's shoulders. Annie and Nathan had their arms around each other. All of them so happy. As if in their wildest dreams they couldn't imagine anything better than being together.

'It's my favourite thing I've ever seen,' Annie said. She was crying quietly.

Ev turned the pages. Al saw the whites of Toby's bones, the shadow of his organs. He remembered Annie saying he was only the size of a plum. He didn't have a name then. He wasn't real. Then Toby just hours old, new to the world. Ruby holding him, her smile almost wider than her face. She looked like the Cheshire Cat. Al wasn't sure he'd ever seen so much joy. Claire sniffled at that one.

'She loved him so much,' Claire whispered, and Ev reached out, squeezed her knee. Someone pulled a packet of tissues out of a pocket, handed them around. There was a photo of Al holding an eighteen-month-old Toby up in the air. He loved it up there, loved to zoom and whoosh. Al could still remember the feeling of the small body in his hands, Toby laughing so much he dribbled right into Al's face.

Ev turned to the very last page.

'Oh my god,' she said and shut the book quickly. 'I can't.'

She handed it to Claire, who opened it, Al reading over her shoulder.

It was an acrostic poem Ruby had written on the inside back cover. Around it, Ruby had painted butterflies and birds in a rainbow of different colours. The poem was written carefully in a girl's neat handwriting.

T reasured boy

O ur lost cousin

B aby so sweet

Y ou are missed so much

Al was surprised by the great blubbering sob that was coming from inside him.

'Honey,' Claire said, and she put her arms around him, squeezed him tight.

'That's the most beautiful thing I've ever seen,' he said over the top of her head, struggling to get the words out as he gasped for breath. He tried to wipe the tears from his cheeks but they kept coming, he couldn't stop them. He stopped trying. Ev passed him the last of the tissues.

Annie walked over and hugged him and hugged Claire. Ev threw her arms around Annie from behind, one hand each on Al and Claire, then Nathan joined in, until they were a mess of tears wetting each other's clothes, their limbs at odd angles like bodies after a crash.

Acknowledgements

MARSHMALLOW WOULDN'T EXIST WITHOUT THE time afforded by the Copyright Agency's Cultural Fund Emergency Action Funding Grant and Creative Victoria's VicArts Grant I received in 2020 and 2021 respectively.

The article referenced on page 244 is 'What Bobby McIlvaine left behind' by Jennifer Senior from *The Atlantic,* September 2021.

The first draft of this book was written at the Wassaic Project in Wassaic, New York, in 2019. I give my endless thanks to the artists I met there and for the opportunity to work on the land of the Mohican and Munsee Lenape Nations. The proceeding drafts were written on the unceded lands of the Wurundjeri Woi Wurrung people. I would like to pay my respect to their Elders past, present, and emerging.

Thank you to Pippa Masson, Caitlan Cooper-Trent and the team at Curtis Brown. To everyone at Hachette, especially Vanessa Radnidge, Louise Stark, Fiona Hazard, Isabel Staas, Maddie Garratt, Eliza Thompson and my patient, generous and brilliant editor, Rebecca Allen. Thanks also to Ali Lavau, Bec Hamilton and Pirooz Jafari. To Alissa Dinallo for the cover design and Chantal Convertini for letting us use another of her beautiful photographs.

To my friends near and far for everything, always. I love you all so much. Special thanks to: Amy Vuleta, Meg Madden, Robert Watkins, Alice Bishop, Alice Robinson, Kate Mildenhall and Leah McIntosh.

RL: you make everything better.

Thank you to my family, especially Dad Han and Katie.

Mum, this one's for you.

Also by Victoria Hannan

When Mina receives an urgent call from her best friend back in Melbourne, her world is turned upside down. Her reclusive mother, Elaine, has left the house for the first time in twelve years.

Mina drops everything to fly home, only to discover that Elaine will not talk about her sudden return to the world, nor why she's spent so much time hiding from it. Their reunion leaves Mina raking through pieces of their painful past in a bid to uncover the truth.

Both tender and fierce, heartbreaking and funny, *Kokomo* is a story about how secrets and love have the power to bring us together and tear us apart.

'An intricate, glittering gem. One of the best debuts in years'
Mark Brandi, author of *Wimmera*, *The Rip* and *The Others*

If you would like to find out more about Hachette Australia,
our authors, upcoming events and new releases, you can visit
our website or our social media channels:

hachette.com.au

HachetteAustralia

HachetteAus